"I run this place, and that's a big job."

"I run a couple of large ranches, but I do find time for relaxation."

"What do you do?"

He looked at her a moment then burst into laughter. "Not much either, I guess, now that you put it that way."

A smile crept to her lips.

"Maybe it's time for both of us to change that." Ross lifted the coffee mug toward his lips. "What do you say?"

Alissa had no idea how to be any different from the way she was. "I'll have to think about that, I guess."

A curious look filled his eyes. "Don't think too long. The idea will just fly away like those butterflies."

GAIL GAYMER MARTIN has had many opportunities to visit the "Salad Bowl" area of the Monterey Peninsula in California, so writing this book was pure joy. Gail feels awed to write stories that honor the Lord and touch people's hearts. With forty contracted books, Gail is a multi-award-winning author published in fiction and nonfiction. Her novels have received numerous national awards, and she has over two and a half million books in print.

Gail, a cofounder of American Christian Fiction Writers, lives in Michigan with her husband, Bob. She enjoys traveling, presenting workshops at conferences, speaking at churches and libraries, and singing as a soloist and member of her church choir where she plays handbells and handchimes. She is also a member of one of the finest Christian chorales in Michigan, the Detroit Lutheran Singers. Visit her Web site at www.gailmartin.com and visit her blog site at www. gailmartin.blogspot.com.

Books by Gail Gaymer Martin

HEARTSONG PRESENTS

HP302—Seasons
HP330—Dreaming of Castles
HP462—Secrets Within
HP489—Over Her Head
HP594—Out on a Limb
HP770—And Baby Makes Five
HP790—Garlic and Roses

Butterfly Trees

Gail Gaymer Martin

Heartsong Presents

To my nieces Andrea Lemon and Jodi Fernandez, who lived on the Monterey Peninsula for years and gave me the opportunity to visit and enjoy this wonderful area. Love and blessings to you both.

A note from the Author:
I love to hear from my readers! You may correspond with me by writing:

Gail Gaymer Martin
Author Relations
PO Box 721
Uhrichsville, OH 44683

ISBN 978-1-60260-068-3

BUTTERFLY TREES

one

An exasperated sigh slipped from Alissa Greening's throat.

The clock's hour hand inched toward the seven as if it were the turtle in the infamous tortoise and hare race. Alissa longed to finish her workday and looked forward to relaxing for the evening, but once again she awaited the late arrival of one of her guests.

She shifted to the registration desk and eyed the registration list. Ross Cahill? Maybe it was Rose. She studied her sister's penmanship then leaned closer and squinted at the nearly illegible scrawl. Fern should have been a physician. Room for two? She shook her head, wishing she'd asked Fern before she'd left earlier in the day. One or two. It didn't really matter. Husband and wife or a single. Either way she had the room ready.

Alissa straightened the pamphlets on the desk, lined her pen parallel to the registration book, then bent beneath the counter to pull out a few more of the monarch butterfly brochures. This time of year, most everyone who registered as a guest at her bed-and-breakfast inn arrived in Pacific Grove to see the phenomenon of the butterflies' migration.

A sound from outside drew her attention toward the entrance. She waited, eyeing the doorway, but no one appeared. Her shoulders sagged, and she turned away, coming face-to-face with one of her guests.

"Do you have any more of those great cookies?" The man's belly lapped over his belt, giving evidence to his enjoyment of food.

"I liked the peanut butter with chocolate chips." He gave her an amiable grin.

5

"They're on the buffet," Alissa said, pointing to the doily-covered cherrywood sideboard she'd inherited from her mother—against her sister's wishes, she could add. Though she tossed off the guilty feelings, it bothered her that Fern had resented their mother's leaving Alissa her antiques.

The man waddled to the buffet, piled a few cookies onto a lace-patterned lavender paper plate and grinned. "My wife will probably eat a few."

"Enjoy them," Alissa said, guessing the wife wouldn't have a chance. She motioned toward the two carafes on the sideboard. "There's tea and decaf coffee if you'd like."

"This is great," he said, lifting the plate in a good-bye salute.

Alissa closed her eyes, wishing she'd thought about cookies earlier. Tonight she'd have to bake another batch, or she'd run short tomorrow. As she turned toward her own quarters, a new sound caught her attention, and as she'd hoped, this time her late guest had arrived.

A well-built man who looked in his forties—about her age—strode through the doorway, pulling two pieces of luggage. His tanned face gave his well-defined features a rugged look.

She sent him a welcoming smile. "Mr. Cahill?"

He nodded without returning a smile. "Sorry we're late."

We're late. Then it was a Mr. and Mrs. At least that's what *we're* made her think. She'd noticed his good looks and apparently had ogled a married man. A sense of guilt slid over her. "It happens. I have your room ready."

A slight frown knitted his brows, but before he spoke, he glanced over his shoulder.

Alissa followed his gaze. Behind him a petite woman stepped through the doorway, her gray hair giving her an air of sophistication, and though Alissa had been taught not to judge others, she did just that when she spotted the woman. "Mrs. Cahill?"

"Yes," she said, a lovely smile filling her face. "Maggie Cahill, and it's all my fault we're late. Ross hates when I—"

She noticed Mr. Cahill roll his eyes, and her back stiffened. Obviously he didn't like waiting on anyone.

"Please, it's not a problem." Alissa gave her a comforting grin, having learned, whether she believed it or not, the customer was always right. "I have your room waiting for you."

She slipped behind the registration desk and turned the book toward the man, but she couldn't stop her gaze gliding from the younger man to the older woman. She realized society looked at things differently now, and May-December marriages were not that uncommon, except in this case the age difference seemed—

"I think there's been a mistake."

His baritone voice jerked Alissa to attention. "A mistake? You are Ross Cahill."

"Yes, but Mrs. Cahill is my mother. We'll need two rooms."

"Mother?" An airy sensation flittered past. "You'll need two rooms." She clamped her jaw closed to keep herself from sounding her frustration. Her sister, Fern, had goofed again. She needed her sister's help, but sometimes Alissa wondered if hiring someone else to fill the part-time position would improve her and Fern's strained relationship. Since Fern needed the money, replacing her would just be another blow. "Let me see." She flipped through the registration book. "I have... No, that won't work." She got a grip on herself. "Yes, I have a room that should be ready, but—"

"Is this a problem?"

Alissa's back straightened with the speed of a switchblade, and she looked into Mr. Cahill's concerned yet very attractive eyes. "Problem?" She tried to control her flush, realizing she had been babbling. "Not at all. I have two rooms, although they aren't together. Whoever took your reservation didn't indicate you needed two rooms." *Whoever.* She knew it was

Fern. She could tell from her hen-scratched penmanship.

"They don't need to be together, dear," Maggie Cahill said, resting her arm on the counter. "I'm sure my son will enjoy the distance."

"Mother." Exasperation filled the man's voice.

Her soft chuckle left Alissa wondering. "Great. I have a lovely room on the first floor if that will work for you, and your room, Mr. Cahill, will be—"

"Ross," he said. "The second floor is fine for me."

She extended the key toward him. "We have no elevator."

"Stairs are fine." He took the key. "I'll help with my mother's lug—"

"Don't bother." Her back stiffened. Did he think she couldn't pull a piece of luggage? "That's my job."

Though his mouth sagged with her abruptness, he didn't argue and headed for the staircase. She watched his agile frame ascend the steps before she walked around the desk and grasped the handle of the woman's luggage. "Let me show you to your room."

"Thank you." Her warm smile contrasted with her son's cold departure.

Alissa pointed down the short hallway. "It's this way, the second room on the right, overlooking the ocean." She'd given Ross a room looking out over the back garden, and now that she'd met him she figured he wouldn't care. In fact, she sensed he'd rather be somewhere else.

Alissa pulled the luggage toward the hallway, beckoning Maggie to follow. "Painted Lady is your room."

"Painted Lady," Maggie repeated as she followed. "You name your rooms. What a lovely idea."

"It seemed fitting. I name them after butterflies." Alissa paused outside the door. "Here we are." She turned the key in the lock, and when she pushed back the door she heard an appreciative gasp.

"It's lovely." Maggie paused again just inside and gestured toward the Victorian furnishings. "Just beautiful. Such lovely shades of blue and white. In the daylight I imagine the view from these windows is glorious. Blue ocean and white waves. Blue sky and white clouds. Truly exceptional." She ambled toward a wingback chair. "Is this an antique?"

"It is." Alissa joined her. "Most of the furniture in this room is from the same era. I love it."

"So do I," she said with a genial smile. "You have a lovely home. The setting is magnificent, and I was drawn to the name—Butterfly Trees Inn. That's why I chose your bed-and-breakfast."

"Really? I'm pleased you chose us." She motioned toward the bay-view window. "We have an excellent location on Ocean View Boulevard. You can watch the seals loll on the rocks, and we're very near Asilomar State Beach for people who enjoy swimming in the summer."

"I do, but I came here for the monarch butterflies."

"They are beautiful. We have many tourists this time of year to see their migration. It's amazing." Alissa dropped her key on the table near the door. "Breakfast is from seven to nine unless you need something earlier. Please let me know."

"Earlier? No. Seven is fine. Thank you so much. I'm here to relax and get some fresh ocean air. My son isn't as excited, but I hope he will be once he's been here a few days. He works too hard. But, you know, mothers aren't supposed to interfere once their children are past eighteen. He's forty-five, but I can't stop myself from being concerned."

Forty-five. Only five years older than Alissa. The immediate calculation gave her an uneasy feeling. She'd never cared about the age of any of her other guests before. The woman's smile drew her back. "You sound like a great mom. I wish I still had mine."

Maggie patted her hand. "I don't feel that way when Ross

bites my head off for making comments. Sometimes he's so quiet, and I know he's under stress. Then he just loses patience, though I'm sure he doesn't mean to. He's so like his father. He has work on his mind all the time."

Alissa didn't know what to say or if she should say anything at all. "He must be stressed."

"Yes, he is." She gave Alissa a smile. "You should have seen Ross and his father clash. They were too much alike when it came to business. Both self-assured and stubborn. My husband could fly off the handle, too, at work, but when he got home and put the work aside, he was the most loving and thoughtful man. I'm hoping this trip will distract Ross and help him relax. My husband had me to distract him. Ross has no one. He's too focused on his work."

"Being in business does that to people." Alissa took a step backward, thinking of her own short temper with Fern. "Have a good rest, and if you'd like some tea or cookies before bed, you'll find them on the buffet in the parlor where you entered. The sitting area is comfortable, and you'll find magazines and a few novels you're welcome to read. My guests leave them when they're finished, so I have a nice collection."

"Thank you, dear. I'm just fine."

Alissa backed away and closed the door softly, chuckling that she'd thought this lovely woman was Ross Cahill's wife. She couldn't imagine his wife having such a gentle personality and friendly smile, living with his abruptness or crabbiness, as his mother had mentioned. As soon as the thought filtered through her mind, she hung her head. *Do not judge, or you'll be judged.* The Bible warned of that.

As she stepped from the hallway, Alissa came to a halt. Ross Cahill sat on the parlor love seat reading a newspaper. She veered toward the desk, hoping to make her getaway. Although she found him attractive, she sensed his personality had the raspiness of a file. Anyway, she had cookies to bake and breakfast to get organized for tomorrow.

"You tucked my mother in?"

Hearing his voice, she spun around, managing to bite back a caustic remark. "I think she can tuck herself in." She added a smile to her clenched-teeth statement.

"I'm joking," he said, folding the paper and laying it aside. "I want to apologize for my grouchiness."

His apology caught her off guard. "That's no—" Yes, it was a problem, but she had to monitor her statement. "We all have bad days."

"It wasn't right to take it out on you. I know better, but sometimes parents can—how should I put it?—bring out the worst in their children. Although we both have to admit, I've long since passed the child stage."

She nodded. "By about twenty-seven years, I'd say, if we define a child from birth to eighteen."

His head drew back, and she could see the glazed look in his eyes. "My mother provided that information, right?"

Alissa grinned, enjoying the sight of his baffled expression changing to acceptance.

"What else did she tell you?"

She moved closer and settled on the edge of an easy chair. "I should plead the fifth or maybe client confidentiality."

"Never mind. I already know. I work too hard, and she worries about me. I didn't want to come here, but I felt obligated. She's a wonderful mother who sometimes drives me nuts."

"She forgot to tell me she's a wonderful mother. The rest is correct."

His eyes widened. "She told you she drives me crazy?"

Alissa laughed aloud at the look on his face. "Not in those words. It was more a subliminal message."

He didn't speak but seemed to study her before a grin grew on his face. "You're an observant woman."

"It's part of running a business. We have to anticipate our guests' needs. . .and thoughts."

"I'd better be careful then."

She felt heat rise up to her neck. "I'd better get busy. Breakfast comes early."

"You do your own cooking?"

"Most of the time. My sister works for me part-time, and during rush season she helps in the kitchen, but I enjoy preparing the meals and baking homemade cookies."

"Cookies?"

She gestured toward the buffet. "Peanut butter with chocolate chips or oatmeal with raisins." Alissa glanced toward the plate, hoping the other enthusiastic guest hadn't wiped the dish clean.

He rose and ambled toward her. "I think I'll say good night to Mom before she falls asleep."

He stood a full head taller than she, and the scent of his aftershave wrapped around her, a heady mixture of cedar and citrus, she suspected. Very manly. When she looked into his eyes, he was staring at her.

"That would be thoughtful, and on the way back, please, help yourself to some cookies." She swung her hand forward and clipped his arm. "I'm sorry." She hurried to her desk and put away the registration book. "You're welcome to coffee or tea, and I have brochures here if you'd like to see a list of activities and sights in the area, and I'd be happy to recommend places for dinner, and—"

"You're tired."

Tired? Alissa heard an amused tone in his voice. Yes, she was tired, but why would he say that? When she looked up, she spotted his crooked grin as he approached the check-in desk.

The answer came to her with his look. "Am I rattling on too much?"

He only chuckled.

Her nerves were showing, and she tried to calm herself for a moment. "I'm sorry. I don't think I properly introduced myself. I'm Alissa. Alissa Greening."

"You're probably tired, Alissa. You've been waiting for us to arrive. You can relax now." He gave her an unexpected grin and headed down the hallway.

Alissa heard his knock on the bedroom door, and she suspected he'd opened the door to say good night to his mother. Maybe he wasn't such a bad son after all. She'd certainly jumped to that conclusion.

Footsteps sounded, and when she looked, he'd ambled over to the buffet and stopped.

His shoulders rose, and he drew in a lengthy breath then shook his head. "I love my mom, but I hate being late. Traveling with her is always an adventure." He grasped a napkin and picked up a peanut butter cookie. "The only thing I like better than these are lemon bars." He took a bite and licked his lips.

The *adventure* comment had caught her interest, and so had the lemon bars. Alissa had a good recipe for those bars. . .if she had all the ingredients. She waited for him to go on, but instead he returned to the buffet and took another cookie. "Are you going to leave me hanging?"

He brushed the crumbs from his lips with the back of his hand. "Hanging?"

"The adventure."

"Oh." He chuckled. "First she called to say she'd gotten hung up at church."

"If you're hung up someplace, church is the best place to be."

He arched a brow. "Not in this case. She met with the pastor to tell him what important point she thought he'd missed during his last sermon."

Alissa sputtered a laugh. "You're kidding?"

"Wish I were."

She loved the sparkle in his eyes, azure eyes like a summer sky, and despite his complaints, she sensed he adored his mother. If not, the man was a great actor. "You said that was first. What was next?"

"We were on the road for twenty-five minutes when she demanded we return home. She'd forgotten her binoculars."

"Binoculars?" Her frown faded. "Never mind. I know. So she can get a closer look at the monarch butterflies."

He glanced at the cookie plate but didn't return for a second helping. "That's why she's here. . .to see butterflies. I could have bought her a big box of her own."

"But that's not the same. These are migrating butterflies that come here year after year. That's really amazing. And beautiful."

"I offered to stop at the nearest town where we could buy another pair, but she would have none of it. These are special ones for butterfly watching my dad gave her for her birthday, his last gift to her."

Alissa's chest constricted. "He died?"

Ross nodded. "He's been gone about three years. They were a team."

"I'm sure it's still hard for her."

He lowered his gaze. "I know. It's difficult for—"

"I still miss my mom, and it's been six years." She'd noticed his distress and had decided to end his pain. "Death is difficult for everyone."

He turned his back and headed toward the coffee carafe.

Alissa watched him pour the coffee into a mug, his head bent as if watching the black liquid proved his greatest challenge for the evening, but she read more beneath his slumped shoulders. Apparently his father's death had made a major impact on him, an unresolved impact.

She busied herself behind the desk, not wanting to invade his privacy, and finally Ross turned and ambled back toward her.

"What kind of activities?"

Her brows tensed then knit as she pondered his question. Feeling the glossy paper beneath her fingers, she caught on and lifted a brochure. "You mean these?"

He nodded and stopped beside her. "If you're tired, please don't let me stop you, and if not, then join me." He motioned toward the comfortable furniture. "At least you can rest your feet while you tell me."

Though she had a multitude of things to do before bedtime, she selected a variety of brochures and followed him across the room. He chose the love seat, and she sat in a nearby chair, hoping to ease the astounding emotion that skittered through her when she stood too near him.

"I'm sure you know what's on Fisherman's Wharf on Cannery Row." She handed him a flier. "It's just up the road, and a major attraction is the aquarium, as well as all the shops and restaurants. The drive along Ocean View Boulevard in the daylight is wonderful. You can watch the seals play on the rocks, and there's Lovers' Point over on—"

Ross's hand rose, and she stopped.

"Alissa." He looked into her eyes. "I hope you don't mind my calling you Alissa."

"Not at all," she said, feeling the familiar heat slip toward her neck.

"I can't relax when you're on the edge of your chair. Can I make you some tea?" He stood and shifted past her. "Plain? Or with something?"

A guest waiting on her. She'd never heard of it. Alissa rose. "You don't have to—"

"You'll never rest tonight if you don't unwind. A cup of tea, decaf naturally, will help you relax."

He didn't listen to her but kept moving toward the urn of hot water. When he had grasped the cup and tea bag, he turned to face her. "Plain or—"

"Plain." She nodded, struggling to keep her mouth from gaping.

Busy filling the mug with hot water, Ross wouldn't see her place the brochures on the low table in front of the love seat. She adjusted a doily beneath a monarch butterfly sculpture and slid back in the chair. A hostess was supposed to offer relaxation to her guests, not the other way around. Her discomfort tightened the cords in her neck.

"Here you go." Ross extended the mug.

Alissa took it and held it between her cupped hands, feeling a tremor in her fingers. She felt like a guest in her own home.

"Now then, let's talk about the activities tomorrow. I'm just riling you, I'm afraid."

She managed a pleasant expression. "I'm fine. Really. Thanks for the tea." She gave a faint nod to the table. "You can take those to your room and look over them. If you have any questions, you can just ask. You know we have tremendous golf courses in the area. Pebble Beach and—"

"I don't golf much, but thanks." He shifted against the cushion.

"I don't either."

He tilted his head. "What do you do for relaxation?"

"Relaxation?" What did she do for relaxation? The question stymied her. Relaxation hadn't found a home in her vocabulary... actually, in her life.

Ross chuckled. "That's not a difficult question."

She lifted her gaze, drawn to his cloudless-sky eyes. "Apparently it is for me. I run this place, and that's a big job."

"I run a couple of large ranches, but I do find time for relaxation."

"What do you do?"

He looked at her a moment then burst into laughter. "Not much either, I guess, now that you put it that way."

A smile crept to her lips.

"Maybe it's time for both of us to change that." Ross lifted the coffee mug toward his lips. "What do you say?"

Alissa had no idea how to be any different from the way she was. "I'll have to think about that, I guess."

A curious look filled his eyes. "Don't think too long. The idea will just fly away like those butterflies."

two

Squinting his eyes against the sunlight edging beneath the window shade, Ross lay in bed and listened to the quiet. He'd had a restless night. Against his will, his thoughts kept slipping to his conversation with Alissa. She seemed so sweet but very nervous, and he wondered why she'd appeared on edge. She had a great business right on the water, and she seemed gifted running it with her cookies, brochures, and amenities he couldn't even remember.

He'd only glanced at the brochures she'd given him, too tired and distracted to concentrate, but he had seen a few things he'd like to do, although doing them alone seemed less interesting than staying home where he should have been managing his ranch.

What do you do? The question tugged his mouth into a grin. He'd asked Alissa the question then had to face his own situation. He didn't do much at all besides work at the ranch. Attending a few social outings here and there, ones he had to attend as a businessman, certainly didn't count. His social life was zilch.

He studied the attractive room. A huge stone fireplace graced one wall, and nearby sat a rocking chair, its oak back etched with a design and a colorful patchwork coverlet draped over one arm. Across the room, an antique armoire towered toward the ceiling, and beside his four-poster bed stood a nightstand that had been a commode table many years ago, he suspected. Throughout, the rich oak wood made the room feel cozy and comfortable. Outside the door, he'd noticed a small oval plaque reading Emperor Room. He grinned. If he were the emperor, he hadn't noticed his royal throne, but he certainly felt like a king with the comfortable bed and even a vase of fresh flowers on the lamp table beside the window.

A door closed, and footsteps thumped past his doorway. Ross turned and glanced at the clock, surprised to see he'd slept until seven thirty. That was unheard of at his ranch. Workers appeared by seven to get into the orchards and fields before the harsh afternoon sun, although the temperature had certainly softened now that October had arrived. Ross slipped his feet over the edge of the bed and rested them on the carpet. He eyed the pleasant room as he stretched his arms out shoulder width with a yawn.

He stood and ambled to the window, lifted the shade, and looked outside. From the view, he realized he had to be at the back of the house. The front and sides would offer views of the ocean. Instead he looked into a courtyard flower garden with a gazebo beyond, and in the distance past the rooftops rose tree-covered foothills of the coastal mountain ranges. He lifted the window and drew in a breath of fresh air. Birdcalls volleyed into the air with their chirps and songs while the birds fluttered their wings in a birdbath or clung to perches of the bird feeders outside.

With their songs in his ears, Ross turned from the window and headed for the shower. The water beat against his back, loosening his tight muscles, and he drew in a lengthy breath of steam as tension washed down the drain. Back in his room, he selected his clothes: a blue-checked shirt with a navy sweater and jeans. He dressed, combed his stubborn hair that he tried to control with gel, then opened the bedroom door.

Before he could step into the hallway, fragrances greeted him—the scent of coffee mingled with the aroma of breakfast sausage. His stomach rumbled, and he recalled that he and his mother had stopped to grab only a bowl of soup on the way up. They were running too late to eat a full dinner, and he'd feared the door would be locked before they arrived at the inn. No room at the inn. The Christmassy thought jumped into his mind, which seemed unwarranted since Christmas was still two and a half months away.

He bounded down the steps, drawn by the tempting scents and the thought of seeing Alissa again. Through an archway, Ross saw the dining room table seated with strangers except for one—his mother, who seemed to be enjoying the company of the other guests. He stepped through the archway, noticing the antique buffet laden with breakfast. He said good morning and lifted a plate, eyeing the fare. Fresh fruit, a sausage casserole—he decided from the scent—muffins, and juice. He filled his plate, poured coffee from the decanter, and settled into a chair beside his mother.

A large man with a protruding belly rose and headed back to the buffet, telling everyone how delicious the casserole was, while a woman who seemed to be his wife encouraged him to leave food for the other guests.

Ross eyed his plate then bowed his head, silently asking the Lord to bless his food and day. When he lifted his gaze, he noticed a few pairs of eyes focused on him. To be polite, he introduced himself then lifted his fork and tasted the sausage dish. The blend of eggs, sausage, bread, and cheese met his hopes, and he had to agree with the rotund man that the casserole was excellent.

His mother lowered her coffee cup. "Did you sleep well?"

He hadn't slept well, not that the accommodations weren't wonderful, but he'd awakened numerous times, thinking of Alissa. He didn't want to go into that with his mother, so he just said, "The bed was very comfortable. And you?"

"Like a baby. I think the sound of the ocean lulled me to sleep."

"I have birds."

"Birds?"

"That's what I hear. My room looks out on the flower garden."

"Flower garden! I'll have to take a walk and see that."

Ross preferred to see the ocean, but he nodded, knowing his mother's love of flowers.

"I suppose the bouquet in my room came from her garden."

"Good possibility," Ross said, forcing his eyes to focus on his mother and not the kitchen door.

When the door finally swung back, he lifted his gaze and readied a smile, but it faded quickly.

"Good morning," the woman said. "You must be Mr. Cahill."

"Ross Cahill."

"I'm glad to meet you. I'm Fern. My sister owns the inn." She extended her hand, and Ross grasped it in his, biting his tongue so he wouldn't ask where her sister was. "If you need anything, just ask."

She shifted to the buffet. Then he watched her leave through the swinging door with an empty serving dish. Sounds came from inside the kitchen, and Ross wondered if the clanging was Alissa cleaning after the breakfast preparation.

The other guests chatted, discussing what they planned for the day and where they lived. His mother added a comment on occasion, but he had no interest in learning anything about the guests. What he wanted to know was Alissa's whereabouts. Four of the guests left, and another followed soon. The only other couple remaining was the overweight gentleman and his wife. The man rose again and returned to the table with a sweet roll.

Ross finished his breakfast and scooted back the chair. "I think I'll read the paper and enjoy my coffee in the parlor," he said. "When do you want to leave?"

"In a bit. I'll finish getting ready, and then I'd enjoy walking through the garden before we go."

"We can do that." He refilled his cup before giving a nod to the other couple and headed into the parlor where he had visited with Alissa the evening before. He sank into a chair cushion and located the newspaper, his gaze shifting from the paper on past the dining room to the kitchen door.

When the telephone rang, his hopes lifted as he focused on the swinging door, but Fern appeared and answered the call. Ross forced himself to look back at the news, feeling disappointed. The emotion didn't sit well with him. He was far too busy to be admiring a woman who lived more than a hundred miles from his ranch.

He paused, captured by the thought. He'd felt a connection to Alissa from the moment he saw her. Something in her eyes—maybe the same kind of loneliness he felt. Yet he hadn't allowed himself to get involved. His work took too much time. *So why*—? Ross drew in a breath. *Lord, is this Your doing? I know You guide our steps, but.* . . He grasped the mug and took a swig of coffee, knowing that what he felt made no sense. He didn't know the woman at all.

"Are you waiting for me?"

His mother's voice pierced his thoughts as she came from the dining room. He dropped the newspaper. "If you're ready, I am."

"I want to read my devotions this morning before we leave, if that's okay."

"That's fine, Mom. I'll go up and make a few calls. How about an hour?"

"Perfect," she said, her smile so gentle that emotion caught in Ross's throat.

He watched her head toward her room, and he took the stairs, thinking that after his phone calls, he might catch a quick nap since he'd had such a restless night.

Inside his room, he checked in with his managers in Paso Robles and San Luis Obispo. He almost felt disappointed everything seemed status quo. No problems. He wasn't missed. Ross shook his head at the ridiculous thought. He should feel relief instead of disappointment.

He set his cell phone on the dresser then plumped the pillow on his bed and stretched out, trying to force his mind into quiet. His brain had other ideas, and after a while, he gave up. His thoughts were one floor down, so he might as well be down there, too.

When he returned to the parlor, quiet had settled over the inn. He heard no sounds from the dining room or kitchen. Most of the tourists were out sightseeing, he guessed. He'd be doing the same soon. He grasped a tourist magazine and flipped through the pages. When he'd settled on an article that had caught his interest, he heard footsteps and saw his mother.

"Are you ready now?"

"Are you?"

"As ready as I'll ever be." He saw the look in her eyes and wished he'd sounded more positive. He added a lighter tone to his voice. "Where are we headed today?"

"Let's visit the garden behind the inn, and then I'd like to head over to the Monarch Butterfly Sanctuary. It's not too far."

"This is your holiday, so I want to do what makes you happy."

She pursed her lips and faced him. "This is our vacation, Ross. I hoped you'd find some pleasure in our trip."

He cringed beneath his mother's words. Didn't honoring his mother mean to respect her and favor her in special ways? Why did he have to be so grudging with his time? He wouldn't have her forever. "What I mean is, I want you to enjoy yourself."

"Then we have the same goal. I want you to enjoy yourself, too." She brushed her hands together as if removing dust.

Her smile had a hint of "I put you in your place," but she always did that with love. After he'd become an adult, Ross realized his mother had to have been a strong woman to deal with his father. Ross and his dad butted heads often, especially as adults in the business. Yet, when he thought about it, at home his father seemed to drop his work at the door and focus on Ross's mother. His mom often said he and his father were too much alike. Maybe that was the problem.

Ross motioned her forward then followed her onto the gingerbread-style porch and down the front steps. The view of the ocean awed him: the rugged rocks and the sun glinting off the waves that dashed in a billow of white foam. The scene tugged pleasure from beneath his internal rock-hard determination to be miserable on this trip as he'd planned. Instead he felt the opposite.

"This is lovely," his mother said, drawing in a breath of air. She closed her eyes, and he could imagine she was remembering times when she and his father had come to Pacific Grove for vacations.

He moved ahead of her down the flagstone path that led to the back of the Victorian house. In the daylight, he noted its lemon yellow clapboard siding with white trim. Its many gables sloped in every direction, giving a mysterious aura of secret nooks and crannies. He chuckled to himself, thinking he'd read too many old classics in college.

His mother's footsteps scuffed behind him on the stone, and when he reached the garden, he paused and waited for her. When she saw the gazebo, she cried out with delight and headed for it. He studied the picturesque summerhouse with its circle of benches and low tables that looked like the setting for a ladies' tea party.

Passing beside colorful autumn blossoms he couldn't identify, except for bushing mum plants and some colorful asters, he mounted the three stairs behind his mother. The gazebo appeared in good condition, no paint chips and recently dusted and swept. The question arose again. Who did all the work?

He hoped Alissa had plenty of help besides her sister, whose smile appeared much less good-natured than Alissa's.

"I love it here," his mother said. "Look at the view—flowers and the foothills—and I can hear the ocean."

When his mother sat on the bench, Ross remained where he was, but when he realized she wasn't planning to move, he sat across from her and waited.

"Good morning."

Ross's neck jerked upward, hearing the feminine voice call from the distance, and his heart gave a lurch when he saw Alissa heading his way.

"Good morning," his mother called while he sat tongue-tied.

In the lamplight last evening, he hadn't noticed the color of her hair. This morning it looked like buttered toast, a blend of tan and gold, appearing so soft in the breeze. Ross liked the short, feathered waves rolling back from her forehead and curving in a soft curl below her ears. Last night Alissa had been amiable yet with an air of business about her. This morning she appeared more carefree and youthful. He'd taken her for his age, but now he guessed she might be younger.

He rose as she approached them with a warm smile on her face. "I wondered if you were away." He wished he'd held back those words. Obviously they meant he'd been looking for her.

"I was tired last night. So this morning, after I prepared breakfast, I had to bake cookies. I usually take care of that the night before." A slight flush colored her cheeks. "I didn't mean to say—"

Ross stopped her. "No need to apologize. I shouldn't have cornered you with all my questions."

"Questions?" His mother's voice lapped over his.

He turned to face her. "I was asking about activities. Alis—Mrs. Greening gave me—"

"Miss, but please call me Alissa."

Miss. Had she never married? He covered his surprise then had second thoughts. Or had her husband died? Perhaps that was the edginess he'd noticed. "Alissa gave us some brochures about activities in the area."

"You don't need brochures." His mother rose and stood beside him while Alissa remained on the grass below. "I've been here many times. I've enjoyed so many things."

"I'm glad," Alissa said, staying where she was. "What have you planned for today?"

"The sanctuary," his mother said before he could respond.

Alissa straightened. "But you don't want to miss the parade. I'm getting ready to go."

"Parade?" Another unison response.

"The second Saturday of October, the school district puts on its annual Butterfly Parade and Bazaar. It's wonderful to see. The children and teachers dress in costumes and parade through town. Have you passed the post office yet?"

"I don't think so," Maggie said, turning a questioning look toward Ross.

He shrugged. "I didn't notice."

"If you're on Lighthouse Avenue, you'll see it. They have a darling bronze statue called the Butterfly Kids. It's two children dressed in their butterfly costumes to commemorate the event."

His mother turned to Ross. "We'll want to see it, too, then."

Ross questioned her remark, but she gave him a hopeful look. He responded with a nod. His goal had been to please her, and the past day had aroused new thinking in his mind. He'd been uncertain that he would enjoy the vacation since his mind kept veering to his business, but now he had second thoughts.

Alissa's enthusiasm seemed on a roll. "After the parade, you'll find a bazaar at the school, and it's great for buying Christmas gifts."

"I'd love to go to the parade. When does it begin?"

"Soon."

"Wonderful. I can go to the sanctuary later." His mother gave him a cursory glance but responded without waiting for his reaction. "May we join you?"

Ross shifted his gaze from his mother to Alissa, trying to anticipate what would result. Though he didn't want to, he liked the idea, and a surprising sense of anticipation waved through him. Yet a parade and bazaar didn't seem like something a man should want to do.

Alissa's face brightened. "Certainly. I'd love for you to come along." She turned toward Ross. "Although I don't suppose you'd be interested."

If he behaved as he normally would at home, he would run from an offer to attend a children's butterfly parade or a bazaar as if his life depended on it. He managed to open his mouth, mustering a playful tenor of a man who really didn't want to go but would. "I suppose I could come along. I've never seen a butterfly parade." He cringed at his mother's questioning look.

"You're not doing this for me, I hope?"

She'd put him on the spot. Now how to respond? He garnered courage. "I'm on vacation, Mom. You told me you wanted me to enjoy myself."

Her look segued to a grin. "That's good."

"Okay," Alissa said, also with a question in her eyes as if she knew she was missing something between them but had to live with it. "Fern just arrived, and she'll take over the inn for me this afternoon. If you wait just a moment, I'll let her know I'm leaving, and we should probably be on our way soon. I'll meet you out front in"—she looked at her watch—"in fifteen minutes." She gave a little wave and bounded across the grass.

Ross watched her go, admiring her guacamole-colored

slacks and matching top with a deeper green trim. But the color also reminded him that if he were at home he would be trying to accomplish a few household chores before he drove to his office in San Luis Obispo to catch up on the avocado business's paperwork. The out-of-his-domain feelings he'd experienced grew to an out-of-his-world sensation. He glanced heavenward and gave the Lord a plaintive look.

ֆ

Alissa grasped her shoulder bag and pulled out her car keys. The excitement rippling through her made little sense. She'd guided people to interesting events before today. So what made the butterfly parade so different? The answer came as her mind filled with the image of Ross's azure eyes crinkled with smile lines—or maybe worry lines—a look that made her want to probe deeper.

Sinking to the edge of her bed, Alissa pictured Ross sitting in the gazebo in the shadows. His hands were folded, his elbows on his knees, his head bent almost like he was praying, but she guessed he was trying to keep his patience while waiting for his mother. Maggie appeared to be a sweet woman yet seemed to grate on Ross's nerves—as parents can—even though God's Word tells Christians to honor their parents. Alissa refocused on her purpose, slipped her feet into walking shoes, and rose. She opened the door to her quarters and headed to the sitting room.

Ross stood near the exit with Maggie nowhere in sight.

"Where's your mother?"

He shrugged. "She can make a simple task into a major project."

Alissa gestured to one of the comfortable chairs. "You'll be on your feet once we get there. You might as well relax."

He eyed the chair and shook his head, his keys jingling in his hand.

Alissa dangled her keys so he could see them. "I'll drive.

I know where I'm going."

A scowl sprang to his face. "I really—"

Determined, Alissa pushed forward. "I'll drive so we don't waste time."

He blanched as a deeper frown knitted his brows, but as he slid his car keys back in his pocket, Alissa wanted to notch one up for herself. She could tell they were both strong willed, and she wondered how that might play out in his days at her inn.

A door closed in the hallway, and in a moment, Maggie appeared in the doorway with a warm smile, a white-haired woman with a youthful air about her. "Are you both waiting for me?"

Ross made a guttural sound. "What do you think we're—"

"There's no problem. We were settling some matters before you arrived." Alissa gave him a don't-you-dare-say-anything look. "We'll take my car. It's a two-door, but I know where we're going."

"Your car? Really?" Maggie flashed a look at Ross, who only shrugged.

She motioned them outside then faced the next battle.

"Mother can sit in front," Ross said, trying to manipulate his long legs into the backseat of her car.

"I will not," Maggie said, squeezing past him. "You're too big, and I prefer being in the backseat." She slipped into the seat with no effort.

Ross settled into the passenger seat and closed the door with an emphatic *thud*. "I'm not used to this."

Though it was a mumble, she'd heard him. "I'm not trying to make you uncomfortable. I thought it would be easier for everyone." She tried to keep her voice hushed, but despite her effort, Maggie, with the hearing of a hawk, overheard her.

"Ross, stop complaining" sailed from the backseat.

Ross opened his mouth to respond then snapped it shut

and chuckled. "I remember Mom complaining when I was the kid sitting in the backseat."

Alissa laughed, too, enjoying his contrite tone. "You'll cherish those memories one day."

"I suppose," he said, settling back and seeming to accept the reality that she was driving.

She found a parking space just off Forest Avenue near Pine Avenue then guided them back toward Lighthouse Avenue, where she hoped they might find seats in the reviewing stand. Ross walked between her and Maggie, and his cedar-and-citrus scent floated toward her on the late morning air.

"This must be a huge event," Ross said. "I can't believe the number of people."

"It's a welcome party for the monarchs. They've begun arriving already, but in another week they'll fill the trees."

"Another week?" He turned to his mother. "Why didn't we come next week?"

"This is a vacation. Your father and I always came for a couple of weeks. There's more to do than the butterflies, although that's my favorite."

His attempt to grin at her left a little to be desired, but Alissa gave him one point for trying.

A few seats remained in the reviewing stand, and Ross climbed first, taking his mother's hand to get her safely seated. When he offered his hand to Alissa, she wanted to evade his touch, knowing how her emotions were playing games with her, but she had little choice. She took it, feeling the pressure of his fingers on hers, his large palm swallowing hers like a protective covering. She sank onto the bench, Ross between her and Maggie, and they settled in.

The children's voices and the noise of the crowd rose, and soon schoolchildren of all ages came into view, costumed as butterflies and monitored by their teachers who'd also dressed for the occasion. A crowd had joined the parade, heading toward Down Elementary School for the bazaar or perhaps for their vehicles.

When the parade had passed them, Alissa rose and Ross followed, putting his hand beneath her elbow as she stepped down then helping his mother to the ground. They joined in behind the parade walking down Fountain Avenue. Ross shifted closer as they walked, his arm brushing against hers. "Yesterday I asked you what you did for relaxation, and I guess this is one of those things?"

She grinned. "Community functions, church activities. I sing in one of the church's praise choirs, for example."

"What do you sing?"

"Praise songs."

He gave her shoulder a nudge with his. "I mean, what part? I'm sure you're not a bass."

She careened a step away from his playful poke. "Alto when they let me. When we're short sopranos, then I'm a soprano."

"Hmm. Versatile as well as talented."

"I'm not sure I'd say that." The sparkle in his eyes nearly undid her.

"Do you sing tomorrow?"

"Our young adult group does. Why? Are you interested in joining us for the service?"

"I think that could be arranged. Mom never misses a service unless she's ill, and she rarely has even a cold."

"You're very welcome to join me. Fern attends a later service so she fills in for me on Sunday morning." She pointed ahead. "You'll see the building. It's not far from the school."

Maggie leaned across Ross. "What are you two talking about?"

"Going to church," Ross said, giving his mother's cheek a pat.

"Good. I thought maybe you were complaining again."

Ross slipped his arm around his mother's shoulders. "Me?

Your son? When do I complain?"

She snickered and wiggled away. "I'll let you demonstrate that for yourself."

Alissa enjoyed the bantering. Playful banter had never been part of her family. Fern's sense of humor was like her mom's, much more serious than Alissa's. Alissa was probably more like her dad, but he'd died in his early fifties, and now he was only a memory. Still, she could hear him laugh at a joke or a comedian on TV. Sometimes he laughed at himself. Her mom hadn't found him that funny, but Alissa recalled she had.

When they reached the school, Alissa led them around the building to the back where the outdoor bazaar was held.

Ross pointed to the banner strung up at the head of the bazaar tables—Butterfly Town, U.S.A. "Is that really what it's called?"

Alissa nodded. "That's our nickname. It's sort of like Gilroy on Highway 101—'The Garlic Capital of the World.'" She turned to Maggie. "Have you ever been there?"

"No, but I've heard of it." Maggie continued to gaze at the colorful banner.

"You should take a ride up there sometime, especially if you enjoy garlic."

Maggie grasped Ross's arm. "Do you hear that? You should take me to Gilroy. Your father never did. I'd like that."

He winked at her. "Anything you say, Mom."

She gave him a playful swat and turned back to Alissa, motioning toward the booths. "Where should we begin?"

"We could split up and then meet if that's easier."

Ross chimed in. "Good idea. I can find a seat somewhere."

"Spoilsport," Alissa said, assuming he was being his usual devil's advocate. "Let's meet by this sign. We can't miss that."

They agreed on a time to meet, and Alissa headed off on her own, stopping to greet people she knew and eyeing items that would make nice gifts. She noted the time; still an hour to go. She continued perusing the booths until she spotted a couple of items for herself, but as she so often did, Alissa hesitated. Her needs were few, but sometimes doodads intrigued her, although her finances often helped her make wise decisions.

"You're empty-handed."

She spun around, hearing Ross's voice so close behind her and noticing his package-free arms. "What about you?"

"Men aren't supposed to buy things, are they?"

"Something nice for your mom, maybe. A remembrance of her trip with you. I'm guessing you don't do this often."

He shrugged. "Not if I can help it."

Alissa shook her head.

"I know," he said. "I can be a jerk. I do really want to please my mother, although I don't suppose I sound like it. She and my dad traveled so much, and they enjoyed each other's company. He was rather headstrong, and she didn't always get what she wanted, so on this trip, I let her pick the location."

"You mentioned your father's deceased."

He nodded. "It's been difficult for Mom."

"Both of my parents are gone. It's because of Mother I have the inn."

"Was the inn her house?"

"No, but she had a nice home and a little savings from Dad's insurance. She left Fern and me everything—except she stipulated the house was mine. She knew I wanted a bed-and-breakfast, and I suppose she thought I'd use it for that."

He looked confused. "But you said the inn wasn't your family home."

Her shoulders knotted as the memories came crashing back. "I sold my mother's house in the downtown area and bought this one with the help of a large loan."

"I suppose that took a lot of faith. Are you happy you did?"

"*I* am. It's been successful, and I keep paying the loan. One day it will be paid back, and the house will be mine."

He gave her a curious look, and she realized she'd said too much. Letting her guests know about her personal problems with Fern wasn't wise. Ross didn't question her, and Alissa didn't offer an explanation.

"Mind if I tag along?" he asked.

"Not at all." The answer flew from her mouth with ease. She'd begun to enjoy his company, and beneath his sometimes abrasive comments, she liked many other qualities she'd seen in him.

He walked beside her as she picked up a few items—a piece of stained glass, a new Christmas wreath for the front door, a hand-knit sweater for Fern in her favorite shades of mauve and blue. Then a metal sculpture caught her eye, and she paused.

Ross seemed intrigued, too, and he purchased a spinning sculpture for his mother to hang from a hook or a tree. "Mom loves her flower garden, so she'll like this."

"It's pretty, and look how it catches the sunlight and seems to change colors." She faltered when she eyed a plant adornment, a metal rod with a monarch butterfly at the top in burnished tones of copper and black.

"That's nice," Ross said, watching her admire the plant stick.

She studied the price tag and set it back. Though the cost wasn't prohibitive, it seemed a waste of money, especially since she'd just mentioned her big loan. With winter coming, the tourist business slowed, and wasting money on thingamabobs seemed foolish.

Ross frowned when she returned it to the display. "You don't like it?"

"I do, but I shouldn't spend the money."

He gazed at the butterfly stick for a moment and then stepped away to follow her.

Alissa headed for a display of stained glass with Ross quiet beside her. She wondered what he was thinking, but since it was none of her business, she turned her attention to prices of the glass items then moved on. When she eyed her watch, she faltered. "I can't believe it, but it's almost time to meet your mom. Are you ready?"

"You go ahead. I saw something back there I want to look at again. I'll meet you in a minute."

He turned away, and she headed for the area where they'd agreed to meet, more and more curious about this stranger who'd become a special person in her life in less than a day.

three

With his eyes on the cross emblazoned in front of him, Ross listened to the Bible verse as God's Word sank into his heart. "And whatsoever ye do, do it heartily, as to the Lord, and not unto men; knowing that of the Lord ye shall receive the reward of the inheritance: for ye serve the Lord Christ." How many times had he heard Colossians 3:23–24? But today the message held a different meaning.

Do it heartily, as to the Lord. He'd thought about good deeds, kindness, and witnessing but never thought of his job, his work on the ranch, in that way. His father had not given his blessing to his decisions, and Ross realized his own pride and spirit of independence had stood between him and his father. Now it was too late to make amends. His father lived in heaven. Still, at times the longing to relent and beg his father's forgiveness smothered him.

He eyed Alissa sitting on the other side of his mother. She looked ahead without blinking, as if she had always worked for the Lord and could reap His reward without hesitation.

Ross lowered his head, studying the nubby-patterned carpet in earthen colors, colors that reminded him of the soil beneath his trees and vines. God watered them with rain, and his business had grown. So why would he even think the Lord didn't approve of his work? The answer rang in his head. *Because my earthly father disapproved, and I was to honor him.*

That was the core of his struggle. Which one to believe, his earthly father who had strong sentiments about what was right and wrong according to the Lord or God's Word that seemed so hard to understand because people tended to put their own spin on the meaning? How convenient to interpret God's Word to fit a person's needs and wants.

Ross rubbed his temple. Had he done that?

The congregation rose and startled him. He'd been too deep in thought to listen to the pastor's final message. Words to the next song flashed on the screen, and the band began to play while people's arms rose in praise as music and words blended into a joyful song to the Lord: "Glorify His Name." Ross sang along, wishing he were closer to Alissa to hear her singing voice. A comfortable feeling washed over him. He did glorify God's name in all he did. At least he hoped he did.

The next song flashed on the screen—"Seek Ye First"—as if the Lord wanted to put a pin in his balloon. The text filled his mind as if affirming his early thoughts. What had he been seeking when he went against his father's advice and bought the vineyard? Was it financial success? Yes and no, but the business seemed to have no relationship to God's Word in Ross's eyes. Why hadn't his father seen that?

In the softer sounds of the song, Alissa's voice drifted to his ears, and a Bible verse pounded in his head. *"Ask, and it shall be given you; seek, and ye shall find; knock, and it shall be opened unto you." Ask.* It seemed so simple yet so late to ask God now what He thought of decisions made and contracts signed too long ago.

Thoughts weighed on Ross's shoulders, and he closed his eyes, wishing the Lord would lift his burden. *Ask. Ask. Ask.* His eyes snapped open. He needed to seek the Lord and ask. It was as simple as that.

Outside in the sunlight, Ross shooed away his darker thoughts. Once again Alissa seemed as lustrous as the morning sun. Her dark blond hair glowed with that buttery beige color he'd noticed before. Today, though, not only her hair sparkled but also her eyes, with light and a dark blue color that made him think of violets. Beautiful eyes to go with her beautiful face.

"You're thoughtful," Alissa said, walking beside him to the car.

He'd insisted on driving today since he'd been on that route for the parade, and he jingled his keys in his hands, wanting to respond but not wanting to be specific. "I guess I am" was all he could think of.

"Did you enjoy the sermon?" she asked.

Enjoy wasn't the word.

"We all needed to hear that message, don't you think?" Her mother's voice jutted between Alissa's question and his attempt to find an appropriate response.

He grinned at her. "That's why it's God's Word," Ross said, grateful for the direction she gave to the conversation.

They all chuckled, and Alissa's question, to his relief, went by the wayside.

He hit the remote, unlocking the car doors, and he helped his mother into the back where she'd wanted to sit again then closed the passenger door for Alissa. As they headed back to the inn, he dug deep to find conversation. "I noticed you've named your guest rooms."

Alissa glanced his way, a crooked grin stealing to her mouth. "They're butterflies."

He thought of the small marker outside his room. "Emperor?"

She nodded. "Yes, emperor is a butterfly as are admiral, viceroy, monarch, mosaic, shasta, angelwing, and painted lady, your mom's room. Each room is named after a kind of butterfly."

"Thanks for letting me be the emperor. I've always wanted to oversee something huge."

"You do," his mother said.

Ross wished she hadn't been listening.

Alissa's eyes widened.

"She means my business," he said to explain.

"What is your business? You've never mentioned it."

"I have an avocado ranch near Santa Barbara in San Luis

Obispo and another ranch in Paso Robles. That's where I live." He winced, waiting for his mother's next comment.

"Avocados. I love them," Alissa said. "They're great in salads, and guacamole is wonderful. Sometimes I put out chips and make it for my guests in the afternoon."

He thanked the Lord for the distraction. "Then you'll have to try my special recipe."

She tilted her head as if to see if he was joking.

"Really. It's great. I'll e-mail it to you when I get home."

Her eyes flickered as if she were still questioning him. "When you get home." She paused. "I'd like that."

Her voice had softened as if she were disappointed, and he wondered if she didn't want to wait that long. "I could call up and see if my housekeeper can find it."

She shook her head. "You don't have to do that." Her face brightened. "Speaking of avocados and guacamole, it's lunchtime. I should get back home and let you eat at one of the great restaurants on the wharf on Cannery Row."

Grasping the opportunity, he let his heart respond. "Would you care to join us?"

"I'd love to, but I need to get back. Fern has plans, and I can't be away much longer."

The hope he'd had fluttered away like dried leaves. "Maybe next time."

"Who knows?" she said, her eyebrows rising.

That wasn't what he wanted to hear. A rousing *yes* or *for sure* would have pleased him. Her *who knows* left him disappointed.

❧

Alissa waved as Ross and Maggie pulled away. An uncomfortable loneliness settled over her. She'd developed a feeling of attachment to Maggie. And Ross? He'd aroused sensations in her that she hadn't felt in years—heart palpitations, pulse skipping, flush rising—foolish and impossible feelings that kept growing.

Using the back door, Alissa slipped inside, expecting the scent of home-baked cookies. Instead she smelled nothing. She dropped her handbag on a kitchen chair and strolled into the parlor and registration area. As she passed the buffet, the scent of freshly brewed coffee wafted past her, and except for Fern on the telephone, the room was empty. She moved closer and peered over Fern's shoulder, watching her chicken scratches entering something in the reservation book.

"Two for October eighteenth," Fern said, making a notation in the book.

Alissa thought of the mess-up with Ross and his mother. "Is that two people or two rooms?"

Fern shot her a frown and dropped the pencil.

Alissa gave her an apologetic look and walked away.

"That's two rooms for the eighteenth," Fern repeated.

Alissa watched Fern's face as she scratched out something in the registration book. "One room. Two people. Good. May I have a credit card to hold the room?"

Alissa headed back to the kitchen, expecting an argument but not wanting one in the guest area. She glanced at the buffet, hoping to see the cookies on the platters along with the coffee. Her shoulders relaxed as she spotted two plates piled with cookies, but as she neared, tension flared. She slipped her fingers beneath the plastic wrap and lifted one. From the feel, she had her answer, and though she had no need to test, she did anyway and took a bite. She knew it. Glowering at Fern's profile, Alissa charged into the kitchen and tossed the store-bought cookie she'd tasted into the wastebasket.

She'd prided herself on nothing but homemade in her bed-and-breakfast. She'd never taken shortcuts, so why had Fern taken it upon herself to bring bought cookies into the inn? Before she could calm herself, the swinging door flew back and Fern stomped into the room.

"You are always questioning me, Alissa, and I'm tired of it."

Alissa raised her hand to calm her, but she noticed her own fingers trembled as she did. "I'm sorry, but I just told you about the misunderstanding with the Cahills' reservation. We have to make sure we understand clearly what the guest wants. Apparently you didn't, because I saw you scratching out the other information."

"If you're going to spy on me, then you need to find someone else to do this job."

Her heart bucking inside her chest, Alissa bit her lip a moment to regulate her tone. "Please, Fern, I don't want to argue. It's Sunday, and—"

"Oh, so no arguing on Sunday, but I suppose Monday through Saturday is fine."

"That's not what I meant." She opened the freezer door and pulled out a few cookies she'd frozen, thinking she'd save them for herself, but now she had no other choice today.

"What are you doing?" Fern swung her hand toward the two plastic containers Alissa had taken from the freezer.

"They're cookies."

"We have cookies. I filled the plates already."

Alissa pried the lid off the first container. Peanut butter. Ross liked those. "They're store-bought. I serve homemade."

Fern put her hand on her hip. "I didn't feel like messing around with baking this morning. As you just reminded me, it's Sunday, and I'm heading for the late service."

"We have aprons. That would protect you from the mess."

Fern flashed a fiery look at Alissa. "These aren't store-bought anyway. They're from a bakery."

"They're still store-bought." Alissa raised her hand again. "Let's stop this now. Please."

"Great." Fern did a dramatic curtsy, grabbed her handbag, and charged out the back door.

Alissa stood there a moment, tears blurring her vision,

before she sank onto a kitchen chair and braced her head in her hands. Why did she get into these verbal attacks with Fern? She wanted to be a good sister, but Fern and she disagreed on so many things. *Lord, You know what I should do. Please give me wisdom and even a hint of what I can do to bring peace to our relationship.*

The prayer hung above her as a chill prickled down her back. Words from Ecclesiastes filled her thoughts. *"Better is the end of a thing than the beginning thereof: and the patient in spirit is better than the proud in spirit."* The verse sank into her mind, leaving her uncertain. The beginning of the verse gave her hope if that was God's purpose in sending her the verse. She sensed the Lord was telling her things would end better than they were now. That's what she wanted.

But what about the last part? *Patience is better than pride.* She'd tried to be patient with Fern. Was Fern's pride getting in her way? Fern had been envious of their mother's bequest. Alissa knew that from day one, but Fern had received a greater portion of the life insurance. She should have been happy, and what had she done with her money besides squander it away? And in such a foolish way at that.

With the questions still nudging her for understanding, Alissa pulled out two crystal platters and filled them with the frozen cookies. By the time any guests came back, she hoped the cookies would be thawed. She carried them into the guest area, replaced the store-bought ones with her homemade ones, and returned to the kitchen. She looked at the cookies and tossed them into the wastebasket. No store-bought cookies for her. She prided herself in homemade.

❧

Ross watched his mother head down the hallway while he let his nose lead him toward the kitchen. The scent of something sweet and lemony filled the air. He glanced at the buffet but saw nothing lemon; then he spied a peanut butter cookie like the one he'd enjoyed the day he arrived. He lifted one and took a bite. As he did, the swinging door flew open, and Alissa strode through, a smudge of flour on her face.

"Something smells good," he said, longing to brush the flour from her cheek.

"I made lemon bars for tonight."

"I love those things."

"I know. You told me." Her expression looked as if she'd just caught herself from stepping into a rabbit hole, and a tinge of pink brightened her expression.

"So I did. Thank you."

She shook her head as if clearing away the cobwebs. "They're for all my guests."

"I know." He opened his mouth to add, *But you knew I love them.* Instead he let well enough alone. She'd already embarrassed herself by telling him as much as she did.

She moved toward the buffet and transferred the cookies from one of the two platters to the other then draped the plastic wrap over the top. "Did you have a nice lunch?"

"We did. We ate at Bubba Gump's. It's a fun place."

"It is. I always chuckle when I see the 'Run Forrest Run' flip cards."

He grinned. "Afterward we sat on the wharf awhile watching the waves roll in."

"Sounds relaxing." She lifted the empty plate.

"It was, and now I'd love a nap, but Mom has other plans."

Alissa laughed, the plate tucked against her slender waist. "And what is that?"

"She wants to go to the butterfly sanctuary. She's in changing from her church clothes, and I'm about to do the same. I can't see looking at trees in dress pants."

He loved her smile. She gave him a nod. "Jeans work better."

"And sneakers."

She grinned. "Well, you'd better get ready, or she'll beat you."

"You're right." He gave her a playful salute and charged up the stairs, feeling heady and confused. He bantered with his mother, but the lighthearted chitchat with Alissa had never been his style. A businessman talked business, usually with businessmen. What did he know about women anymore? That hobby—and he knew he called it that in self-defense— had been put on a shelf like model cars and video games.

He used the key and pushed open his bedroom door. The flowers still stood on the table, but beside them, he spotted a bowl of fruit—an apple, an orange, a banana, and a plum. *Nice touch.* Alissa had added so many nice amenities to her inn, including those wonderful home-baked goodies.

He slipped off his shoes and tossed himself onto the bed, closing his eyes a moment to sort out his thoughts. His ranches needed attention, he knew, but for the first time in his life, he didn't want to contact anyone to find out what new problems had arisen, if any. They had his cell phone number in case of an emergency. Since he'd bought the vineyard, his life had revolved around work. Running two different produce ranches kept him hopping. His father had told him that, among other things, but his wealth had grown as he thought it would.

Wealth. What good was it in the bank? He reinvested, but otherwise it was just piling up. No wife to leave it to, no children to benefit. He'd leave his money to his church perhaps, or. . . He pulled a pillow from beneath the bedspread and tossed it over his face. *Stop thinking about death and bequeathals.* It was too depressing.

His father filled his mind again, and Roger. . .his brother.

He tossed the pillow to the foot of the bed and raised himself on his elbows. Outside was a blue sky with promises of a bright day, a pleasant day, so why had he filled his mind with gloom and doom?

Ross rose and slipped off his dress pants, hung them over

the rocking chair, and grasped his jeans from a chair, though he'd left them on the floor. He figured Alissa hadn't cleaned his room, but in case she ever did, he needed to be more careful. Neater for sure. He tugged off his shirt and grabbed a knit pullover from a dresser drawer where he'd tossed his folded clothes. Tucking his shirt into his pants, he did a balancing act while slipping on his shoes. A mirror reflected his image—hair messed and a hint of a five o'clock shadow. Before going down, he grabbed his shaving kit and headed into the bathroom.

&

Hearing someone in the other room, Alissa left her pan of lemon bars and stepped through the swinging door. Maggie stood beside the coffeepot as if considering whether she wanted a cup. "Would you like some tea instead?" She motioned inside the kitchen. "I have water on the stove."

"Thanks, but I suppose I don't need anything. We had a lovely lunch."

"Ross told me, and he said you're going over to the Monarch Butterfly Sanctuary now."

"We are." She gave a little nod, but her eyes looked past Alissa into the kitchen.

Alissa guessed at her thoughts. "Would you like to look around?" She motioned inside.

"I'd love to." Her steps quickened as she passed through the doorway and stopped. "This is so nice. Everything so clean and bright, and look at those." She pointed to the lemon bars. "Ross loves those things."

"Yes, I—yes, he told me earlier."

Her eyes softened when she looked at Alissa. "He's a good son. Ross. I'm proud of him."

"I'm sure you are. He's a successful businessman, and that would make any mother proud."

"You never had children?"

"I never married. Time ran away with itself. I dated a few

nice gentlemen, but I never met anyone I'd consider a soul mate, and I never felt the Lord encouraging me to give my heart to any of them."

"God will bless that strong faith," Maggie said, resting her hand on Alissa's. "And don't give up. You never know when that special someone will appear in your life. One day you'll feel an immediate connection and. . ."

Though Alissa heard the rest of Maggie's comments in the periphery of her mind, she felt frozen to the floor. That exact feeling had washed over her the day she'd met Ross. He'd been irritating and cool, but when they'd talked later after his apology, she sensed a connection, a strange sensation that they'd known each other forever. The emotion seemed so foolish under the circumstances. She'd just learned his name, and she saw his eyes. How could anyone recognize a soul mate based on that little bit of information?

But she had.

"Ross is an only child?" Alissa asked, forcing herself to concentrate.

Maggie's face darkened. "No, he had a younger brother." She closed her eyes. "Roger."

"I'm sorry. Had he been ill?"

"Yes, but not in the way we think of illness."

Alissa felt herself frown, confused by Maggie's comment. "Was it a rare disease?" She shouldn't probe, but her desire to know more about the Cahills overshadowed good sense.

"It's very common. Roger died in a car accident. A drunk driver accident."

"That's so tragic."

"Our faith is strong, and we chose not to drink alcohol in our family."

"I understand. I've never indulged either. It's safer that way. Alcoholism sneaks up on people without their even realizing it."

Maggie's head lowered. "It does, and no matter what a

family does, it doesn't help."

"Alcoholics need the Lord," Alissa said, hoping to soothe the woman's sorrow. "Did the driver die in the crash? So often they survive."

Maggie's head lifted, her eyes glazed. "Roger was the drunk driver. He killed a mother and her child." Maggie rested her cheek against her hand. "It's difficult to forgive him for that."

Air escaped Alissa's chest as if she'd been kicked in the stomach. Maggie's tone, so harsh and bitter, seemed out of place coming from this gentle woman. Alissa struggled for words of comfort. "But we must forgive."

She opened her arms, and Maggie melted into her embrace. They stood there until Alissa heard Ross's footsteps on the stairs. Was this the dark shadow she'd witnessed in his eyes when he didn't realize she was looking? Feeling guilt for someone else's sin seemed natural when it came to family. She thought of her relationship with Fern and faced the truth. She'd never felt guilt for her sister's envy. Maybe it was time to put herself in Fern's shoes.

"Thank you," Maggie said. "I don't talk about that often, and maybe I should." She stepped back and pushed open the swinging door.

Through it, Alissa saw Ross standing near the registration desk, his hands in his pockets, looking toward the outside door. Across the highway, the ocean sprawled before them, dashing against the rocks as if trying to shatter the hard stone. Life seemed that way. Waves of guilt, fear, and sadness lashed against life's stability, and only a rock could endure the usual corrosion that destroyed life's beauty.

Alissa knew she had her Rock, her Savior, but how often she found herself wallowing in the waves without clinging to the Rock for support. How long did it take God's children to trust in Him and believe His promises? *He is my Rock and Fortress,* she reminded herself.

four

"Fern, we have to talk." Alissa gripped the telephone receiver, managing to keep her voice under control.

"I think you said all you needed to say yesterday, Alissa. I'm looking for another job."

Alissa blinked back her surprise. She hadn't expected her sister to go this far; she needed to get the conflict under control, and now. "Please reconsider. I can't leave here, so could you come over? Let's talk and see how we can resolve this. You're my sister, and I love you. I'm sorry for hurting your feelings."

The line was silent, and Alissa held her breath for a moment.

"This wasn't the first time, you know. I can't seem to please you. You have your ways, and I'm different. I do my best, but apparently I'm not perfect."

"I'm not perfect either, Fern. I'm so far from it. I made a mistake, and I want to talk about it but not on the phone. Please stop by."

More silence.

"I'll come over later. I have an appointment this morning."

The telephone clicked and went dead. An appointment? Was her appointment regarding a job? Alissa recalled how many times she'd asked herself, even the Lord, if she should let her sister go and hire someone else. Now was her chance, so why did she feel so guilty?

With the receiver still pressed to her ear, Alissa was provoked by the sound of a dial tone and dropped the receiver onto the cradle. She turned and braced her arms against the kitchen island. Had this been her fault? Did she expect too much from

Fern? Her thoughts flew back to months after their mother's death when they'd reached a peak of stress. She and Fern both dealt with her death in different ways. While Alissa turned inward, Fern took her inheritance and went on a spending spree. Worse than that, the image of a man Fern had met filled Alissa's mind. Anger prickled up her back. How could Fern have been so stupid? She forced the image from her mind, wanting to forget the disaster that had followed.

Awareness replaced the prickle along her back. Alissa knew she had harbored resentment and frustration with Fern during this time. She'd behaved like a teenager who'd been released from her curfew and given too much money to spend. Fern had done everything that went against her better judgment then came back hangdog, wanting forgiveness. Though it was hard, Alissa had granted it.

Or had she?

Forgiveness. The word roared in her ears like a Harley revving outside her door. She'd told Fern she'd forgiven her, but now she wondered if she had. Or had she just begun treating her as if she were a little slow-witted and needed to be pitied?

Fern had made one major mistake, but Alissa looked into her own past and asked herself if she'd been perfect. Never. Not if she were honest. Alissa had asked the Lord to forgive her sins, and she believed He had. Fern had believed her, too, but unlike God who was faithful and true, Alissa realized today she had failed her sister.

"Hello."

Ross's voice sailed through the kitchen door, followed by his tap. Every time she heard his voice, her heart did a jig and she had to steady herself. She pushed open the door. "Looking for those lemon bars?"

He grinned. "Now that you mention it."

She opened the door farther and motioned him inside.

When he stepped in, he paused and looked around. "So this is where you do all your cooking magic. You make the best of everything."

"I think that's stretching it a little, but thank you."

He rested his hand on her shoulder. "Nice place you have here. It even smells good."

So did he, she thought. The warmth of his palm radiated down her arm, and heat rose to her cheeks. She knew she was blushing again, so she moved past him toward the refrigerator where she'd placed a tray of lemon bars. She pulled it out and turned back the wrapper. "Would you like one?"

His hand shot forward almost before she'd finished asking. "How could I refuse? These are my favorite."

I know clung to her lips, but she held back the admission. She didn't want to cause herself any more embarrassment as she had with his mother. "How was your day?"

He lowered the lemon bar. "Mother had a wonderful time."

Alissa placed the tray on the kitchen island and picked up a bar for herself. "That's not what I asked." She took a bite, enjoying the sweet-sour tang that pinched her cheeks.

He shook his head as if upset with himself. "It was okay. We took a drive north and then back to the sanctuary again. Today we did see monarchs, but not as many as Mom hoped. At least it was more than yesterday afternoon. I suppose the trees will be filled with them soon enough."

"Next week it will be glorious. Did you bring a camera from home?"

"I think Mom brought one."

"Be sure to take photos. I've known people who've had them enlarged and framed and used them in their homes as artwork. It's a magnificent sight."

His gaze searched hers for a moment as her discomfort built.

"I'm sure it is," he said, his voice sounding throaty.

His heady aftershave enveloped her, and she wanted to turn from the searching look in his eyes. "I should buy one of those photos and hang it in the parlor." Her voice sounded foreign and far away.

He didn't say anything.

"Photos can make. . ." Alissa caught herself rambling again with her uneasiness. "I suppose I'd better get some plates filled and the coffee out there for the guests' afternoon snack."

"Then I should let you work." Ross straightened and took the last bite of his lemon bar then pulled a napkin from the holder on the island and wiped his fingers. "Mom's taking a nap, I think, and I'm going to—"

Before he could finish, Maggie called to Alissa from the other side of the door.

Ross pushed it open, and Maggie smiled at them, holding a large bag imprinted with GARLIC GARDEN.

"So you went to Gilroy, too."

Maggie stepped toward her. "We did, and I couldn't resist buying you a present for your pretty kitchen."

She handed Alissa the gift, and she opened it to find a long garlic braid inside. "Decoration? I can hang it right here, but I'll cook with it, too. These garlic buds are usable."

"I know." Maggie grinned. "And it lasts a long time, the clerk said."

Alissa opened her arms. "Thank you so much. This was very thoughtful."

Maggie embraced her then backed away. "Now I want to have a short nap. Ross is taking me out to dinner." She gave Ross a strange little look then scurried away.

Ross caught the door and paused. "I'll let you get back to work, as I said earlier. I think I'll sit out there and read the paper."

"I have a flavored coffee today. Try it, and let me know what you think."

He agreed and slipped through the swinging door while she watched it sway back and forth a moment and tried to collect herself.

Getting a grip, Alissa placed the bars on a decorative plate and grasped a carafe of flavored coffee then followed Ross into the parlor area. After she set the carafe and dish on the buffet, she glanced toward Ross. He'd leaned back, his nose buried in the *U.S. World News*, and she noticed he'd slipped off his shoes and propped his feet on the crossbars of the table in front of the love seat. He looked relaxed and content; Alissa wished she could feel that way, but her problem with Fern still hung in front of her like a carrot. It had become her driving force.

She ambled into the seating area and straightened the magazines, checked the flowers for freshness—they needed redoing—and picked up a paper plate and empty cup sitting on a table. As she turned, Ross spoke to her from behind his reading.

"I notice you had fewer guests today."

She looked at the back of the newspaper. "This time of year, our guests often check out on Sunday or Monday morning, and then we're busy again starting Thursday night or Friday and through the weekend."

He lowered the paper and looked into her eyes. "Then that gives you some free time to enjoy yourself."

She shrugged. "A little, I guess, but someone still needs to be here."

"What about Fern?"

Fern. A knot tightened in her neck. "My sister's been doing some other things, but, yes, she does come in to help when I need her."

"Are you free this evening?"

His question startled her. "I—I. . . What do you mean?"

He folded the paper and placed it beside him. "I thought maybe you'd like to join us for dinner. We want to go into

Monterey to find someplace interesting to eat, and you could help us pick a good one."

"I can do that," she said, hearing a tremor in her voice. She tried to rehear what he'd said. Had he actually asked her to dinner?

"You can join us? Great." He sent her a broad smile.

"No. . .ah, I don't know about that. I meant I can help you find a good restaurant."

His smile faded. "You can't go with us? Mother will be disappointed. She thought it was a good idea."

His mother. Her nervous anticipation was swept away like crumbs beside the buffet. His mother had wanted him to ask her. She heard herself chuckle and tried to stop, but everything seemed so ludicrous.

"Did I say something funny?"

Alissa grasped her decorum and struggled to tame her giddy feeling. "I wasn't laughing at you. I laughed at myself."

He tugged at the collar of his polo shirt. "I'm glad to hear that. No one ever accused me of being humorous."

"But you are, you know. You've made me laugh more than once."

He tipped his head. "Thank you for the unexpected compliment. Let me know when one of those moments happens. I want to cherish it."

She laughed at his silliness, happy for the release from her personal gloom. "How about just now?"

He shook his head, a grin stealing to his face, but it was short lasting. He became serious again. "If you change your mind, let me know. It would make my mom very happy."

"Thanks." She backed up a step, wanting so badly to sit and talk with him about her struggles with Fern, but it wasn't right. People just didn't open their hearts to a customer. "I doubt if I could get help for tonight." She took another step backward. "Maybe another time."

He gazed at her a moment, his look probing, then tossed her an accepting nod, leaned back, and picked up the newspaper again. "I'll be right here."

Alissa strode back into the kitchen, set the coffee mug in the dishwasher, and tossed the paper plate in the trash. She opened a drawer and grasped the scissors she used in the garden then slipped out the back door. Right now she needed some air and time to think, but as well she wanted to refresh the parlor flowers.

She headed into the garden and studied the flowers in bloom. The stock was beautiful, and she loved the scent. She gathered a mixture of white, rose, and purple flowers, cutting the stems long for the vase, and then moved to the foxgloves, their tiny trumpets in a deep purplish pink playing off the multihued stock. She thought of the mums, hoping she might find some with stems long enough to work with the ones she'd already cut. As she turned toward them, she faltered.

Ross headed across the grass toward her. "Very nice," he said, eyeing the flowers then gazing into her eyes.

She melted at the sound of his voice. Her mind reeled as she tried to decipher what power this man held over her. "The parlor needed a pick-me-up."

He stepped toward the gazebo. "So do you, I think." He motioned for her to follow.

She eyed the bouquet in her arms, knowing the flowers needed to get into water soon, but despite her excuse, she turned and moved toward the gazebo.

Ross sank onto a bench and patted a seat alongside him. "I know those flowers need to get inside, but I have a question, and I'd prefer to talk in private. Some of your guests have already come back for the afternoon."

Her chest tightened with his admission. *Private?* What did he want to know that needed privacy? If he wanted to know about good restaurants, she could give him some ideas about them in front of the guests, but she sensed his question was more personal. Confused, she sank beside him on the bench. "How did you know I was out here?"

"Lucky guess." He gave her a crooked smile. "I tapped on the kitchen door—I knew you'd gone in and you hadn't come out—and you didn't answer. Then I recalled you'd looked at the flowers earlier in the guest area so I added two and two."

A grin sneaked to her mouth. "You're quite the detective."

"Only when it's an important case."

Important case? She managed not to frown. "Okay, Sam. What's the question?"

"Sam?"

"Sam Spade." She'd say anything wacky to lighten her heart.

"Ah." He rested his elbows on his knees and folded his hands, his head lowered.

His seriousness gave her pause. "Did I do something wrong?"

He tilted his head upward to look at her. "Nothing at all, but something is wrong."

"Your room? I'll talk to the cleaning lady."

"It's not the room, Alissa. Something's up with you. You're not yourself." He gave her a look she didn't understand. "I know we've only known each other for a few days, but that's long enough to see someone's heart, and yours isn't in it today. Something's wrong."

She gave a nod, amazed he'd sensed that, knowing her for such a short time. "Yes, Your Honor, that's true."

" 'Detective,' remember. You don't have to call me 'Your Honor.' "

A grin tugged at her cheek. "It's complex and nothing I should share with a guest."

"I don't expect you to open your soul. I just thought maybe I could help."

She shook her head. "It's something I have to do." Alissa

drew in a deep breath, longing to talk with someone. "In short, I had an argument with my sister, and she's quit."

"Quit." His eyes widened. "Then you're in a bind."

"With very tight ropes."

"Any hope of patching things up?"

Alissa turned sideways and placed the flowers on the other side of the bench beside her. "I've asked her to come over tonight and talk."

"Do you know how to make things better?"

"The problem's been a long time coming. Right now all I can do is apologize from the bottom of my heart, ask her forgiveness, and hope we can come to an understanding."

"Sounds like a good plan." He shifted on the bench to face her more fully. "And you can pray."

"I've done that, but you know, I realized today that I've brought some of this on myself. I've been blaming Fern, and I think I'm carrying some old grudges that really need to be tossed in the trash can." She massaged the stress in her neck. "Doing that will be more difficult than admitting it."

He rested his hand on her arm. "It always is, but it's worth the try. And with God's help, things are possible despite our doubts."

"I know." She felt more at ease talking with him than she'd expected. Ross had a tender way about him, his voice gentle, his eyes sincere. She turned her neck back and forth, relieving the tension.

Ross lifted his hand and rested it on her neck. She felt his strong fingers massage her taut muscles while a warm, wonderful sensation whispered along her skin. "Thank you. That was nice."

He lowered his hands. "I hope I wasn't too forward. I can see you're stressed."

Alissa eyed the flowers and the time then gathered the bouquet in her arms. "Have a nice time at dinner with your mom, and maybe one day I can please her by joining you for dinner."

He placed his hand on her arm again. "It would please me, too, Alissa. Very much."

Astounded at her growing feelings, she rose, holding the bouquet to her chest. "I'd better get these in water." She descended the three steps to the ground. "If you want to go somewhere with good seafood, you could try Passionfish up on Lighthouse Avenue in Pacific Grove, or for steaks, try the Whaling Station in Monterey. I can give you directions." She gave him a wave and headed inside, her heart and mind battling with the feelings she'd discovered so recently.

Inside the kitchen, she paused, and in the hush, Alissa prayed. "Lord, help me to understand what's going on with my emotions. Is this You or just passion sneaking from the chambers of my heart? Help me to know the difference. You know this scares me, but I want to put my trust in You."

&

In her apartment, Alissa heard footsteps outside her door. When the knob turned, she knew it was Fern. Her sister gave a quiet rap on the doorjamb then swung it open.

"Come in," Alissa said, not needing to since Fern had already stepped over the threshold. "Thanks for coming. It means a lot to me."

A slight frown wrinkled her sister's brow. "You're welcome."

Alissa felt tongue-tied. "How did the appointment go?" Bad question, but it was out.

"I had my hair trimmed." She reached up and touched it.

Relief washed over Alissa as she saw her sister's shorter hair. "It looks nice. I like it." She motioned to a chair. "Have a seat. Can I get you something to drink?"

"No. I'm fine." Fern eased into the chair and finally leaned back. "What do you want to talk about?"

"Us."

The room fell silent, and Alissa tore into her confused thoughts to come up with the right thing to say. All her thinking that afternoon had twisted her stomach into a knot.

"Okay," Fern said, not adding anything else.

Alissa grasped her careening thoughts clashing in her mind and tried to put them in order. "First I want to apologize. I have been critical, and I need to monitor that. You know how important this business is to me, but you're more important, Fern. We're sisters."

Fern's head shot up as if she'd been bopped by a tennis ball. "We are, but I realize this is your business and I'm an employee."

"That doesn't excuse my behavior. We need to decide what's really important to the business and how we can work together without having this happen." Honesty struggled up from the depths of her heart. "I started thinking today about what I've been doing. I keep going into the mistakes you made in the past, I think—but please know I've made many of my own—and I'm not giving you credit for maturity and wisdom. I'm also not doing what I said and forgiving you for losing so much of your inheritance. It's really not my business, and it's not fair to you."

Fern sat quietly, but Alissa could almost see her mind sifting through what she'd said. She finally lifted her gaze. "Thank you." She fidgeted a moment before continuing. "I'll admit I've made mistakes, too. I know it's important to get the registration right. I was careless the other day when I messed up the one for the Cahills. I'm happy you had the room. I would have truly made a problem for you if the room hadn't been available."

Alissa studied her sister's repentant face. "I think the Lord looked over that situation. I'm sorry about the cookies. I pride myself in having only homemade, but I can't expect you to do the baking. You did what you thought was right and bought them from a bakery. I'm sure they were like homemade, but it was my pride."

"I'll try to remember how important it is to you, Alissa, but you know, I've been thinking. Maybe I should strike out on my own. I can't be dependent on you all my life. It will just add to your resentment. I had money, and if I'd been careful, I would still have a savings and finances to fall back on, rather than need income to supplement what I wasted."

What he wasted filled Alissa's mind, but she muzzled the thought. "It's reassuring when you're here. I know you're family, and I can count on you to be honest and to treat people well. You've always done that. Anyway you're my sister."

"But that shouldn't be your purpose in having me here. If I'm not doing the job you want, then I should be asked to leave."

"I don't want you to leave. I think we can work this out. It's good for me to soften my criticism. I handled the cleaning lady who messed up a few things better than I handled you."

Fern's mouth turned upward in a slight grin. "That's because we're family, and we have to love each other."

Alissa rose and put her arms around her sister's shoulders. "We don't have to love each other, but we do."

"We do," Fern said, returning her hug.

"Can we pray together, Fern? How long has it been since we bowed our heads together anywhere other than for a blessing at a meal?"

"A long, long time."

Alissa sat on the arm of the chair and joined hands with Fern. They closed their eyes and bowed their heads, asking the Lord to bless their relationship and to give them wisdom to handle problems before they got out of hand. At the end of the prayer, she raised her head and saw moisture in Fern's eyes and felt tears in her own. She loved her sister, and Fern loved her. With God's help, they could make things right.

five

Ross bounded down the stairs, hoping to see Fern helping with breakfast, but when he turned toward the dining area, Alissa was at the buffet. His pulse gave a jolt, sensing nothing had been resolved between them in their talk the past evening.

He stepped behind her and reached around for a coffee mug.

Alissa jumped, and when she looked at him, a smile lit her face. "Good morning. Did you sleep well?"

He gave a perfunctory nod, surprised at her bright smile. "How about you?"

"The best sleep I've had in a couple of days, thank you."

His mind billowed with curiosity, but with other guests were sitting at the table, she'd shifted to a more business-like manner. He filled a mug and eyed the fare for the day: cheese melted on English muffins and topped with a strip of bacon. Then he noticed a great-looking fruit cobbler. As he dished a muffin and some fruit on his plate, he heard his mother's voice.

"Good morning, everyone," she said, smiling at those seated as she headed Ross's way. She veered past him and stopped beside Alissa. "Thank you for the wonderful restaurant suggestions. We enjoyed the steak so much. It was very tender." She leaned closer and spoke in a hushed voice. "I'm sorry you couldn't join us. We thought we'd try the other restaurant tonight. Any hope of—"

Ross pressed his hand against her arm, keeping his voice hushed. "Alissa might not have anyone—"

"I'd love to join you. Fern will take over tonight." She gave Ross an arched-brow look followed by a grin.

His mother pressed Alissa's hand in hers. "Wonderful. I'm so pleased." She glanced at Ross. "About seven?"

Alissa nodded and slipped back into the kitchen.

Ross settled at the table and took his first bite. The muffin was excellent, and today he thought he might behave like the big dude who went back for seconds a couple of mornings ago. Before his second taste, his cell phone chimed. Disappointed, he let the muffin drop to his plate and grasped his phone. "Excuse me," he said, flipping it open as he walked into the parlor. "Ross Cahill."

He sank into a chair, hearing the manager he'd left in charge relate a contract problem with one of their largest distributors.

"Give me his number. I'll call him from here. If we need to talk in person, I'll have to drive back for a day." He grabbed a notepad from the registration desk and jotted down the number. "Thanks, Hersh. Is everything else okay?"

He listened to his manager's calm voice.

"Great. I'll get back to you."

After he hung up, he started to make the call then flipped the cell phone closed. No sense in ruining his breakfast totally. He might as well eat first and fight later. Ross slipped the phone back into his pocket and headed back into the dining room. When he'd settled down with his breakfast, his mother leaned closer, a worried look on her face.

"Problems?"

He shrugged. "Nothing a telephone call can't resolve, I hope. I'll call after breakfast." He sank back against the chair, but the food didn't sit well. Problems with distribution could be serious. The product made it to the market through distributors and no other way. Avocados needed to reach stores at their peak—not overripe.

His mother rose to refill her coffee cup and take a little more fruit cobbler then sat again. Ross sensed her watching him, and he tried to relax his expression. "Are you anxious to get to the sanctuary?"

"When you're ready."

"I shouldn't be too long. If it's a problem, then I'll go to Plan B."

"Plan B?"

"Let's stick with Plan A for now, Mom." He slid back his chair and carried his cup to the decanter. "I think I'll take a walk outside and make the call."

His mother gave an agreeable nod, but he spotted concern on her face. The sooner he resolved the situation, the better.

"Are you going to the sanctuary?"

Ross lifted his gaze to an elderly woman seated at the end of the table.

His mother's concern shifted to an amiable smile. "We are once my son's business is finished."

"I'm heading that way. I'd be happy to take you over with me. I just have to get my binoculars, and I'm ready."

"That's so kind." She turned to Ross. "Would that be helpful, Ross?"

He wanted to kiss the woman across the table. "That would be great, if you don't mind."

The woman smiled. "I'd be happy to have someone to go with. I'm Amanda Darling." She shook her head. "I know. It's a strange last name, but my husband was as delightful as the word. He was darling."

"You're a widow?" Maggie asked.

Amanda nodded. "For two years. It's difficult."

"Ralph's been gone three years. We have a lot in common."

Ross felt as if he were an onlooker in the female conversation. "If you're settled, then I'll go ahead and take care of business."

"That would be wonderful, and you can pick me up about—" She eyed her watch.

"No need," Amanda said. "I'll be coming back. Are you on a time schedule?"

His mother waved him away. "None at all. I'm sure my son would be grateful."

Ross leaned over and kissed his mother's cheek then turned to Amanda. "Thank you. Have a great day, Mom, and I'll see you later."

"I'll be back by dinnertime," she said.

He gave her a thumbs-up and headed outside, filled with a sense of freedom. He'd been a dutiful son the past few days, but today with the added problems at the ranch, he could use some breathing space. He strode to the gazebo and slid onto a bench. In the shade, the morning breeze drifted in and ruffled his hair. He pulled the paper from his pocket and eyed the number, but before hitting the buttons, he gave thought to the problem and how he might solve it. He had an ominous sense he was being more positive than he would feel when he ended the conversation.

After thinking it through, he punched in the number and waited. "Chuck Conklin, please," he said when the secretary picked up. Silence reigned over the line except for ghostlike voices far in the distance echoing from other calls somewhere along the cables. Finally a gruff "Hello" cut through the sound.

"Chuck, this is Ross Cahill. I understand—"

Ross's eyes blinked when he heard Chuck's contentious tone that followed.

"I know what our contract says—"

With his mind spinning, Ross listened to threats from his largest distributor. "You know weather conditions affect our crops. Who else has met their contracts this year in California?"

More intimidation followed.

"So what's our solution?" Ross already knew. The guy wanted

to raise prices and at the worst time when his crop had been affected by things out of his control. "We all have to make a living, Chuck."

Ross realized the conversation was going nowhere. He needed to look at the books and see the guy in person. A telephone conversation wouldn't resolve this issue to his satisfaction at all. When Chuck quieted, Ross took over. "I need to talk with the manager and see what we can do to resolve this. We're happy with your service, and I understand you have employees to pay, too. What works best for you, San Luis Obispo or Paso Robles?"

Though he grunted a response, Ross sensed a face-to-face meeting was what Chuck wanted. Chuck had made it clear he expected Ross either to meet the contract or to provide him with some compensation. That would mean a new contract, which was what the guy was hoping for, Ross realized. "How about tomorrow afternoon at my office in San Luis Obispo? Say around one."

Chuck agreed, and Ross ended the conversation, knowing he needed to call his manager before giving any thought to contract concessions. He slipped his cell phone into his pocket and rose from the gazebo bench.

The morning held the promise of another beautiful day, and instead of worrying about his business, Ross wished he could head to a park or walk on the wharf, anything but have stress follow him here. The surroundings of Pacific Grove offered nature in all its glory—the rolling waves dashing against the seal-laden rocks, the bay's white foam spreading along the beach, and the colorful monarch butterflies clinging in clumps on the eucalyptus and pine trees. But the beauty didn't linger in Ross's thoughts. Instead his mind settled on his problem and clung to the hope that he could find the wisdom to deal with Chuck.

He trod across the yard, and as he reached the house, the

back door opened and Alissa stepped out. "I see you escaped visiting the butterflies today."

"And I'm grateful. A woman at breakfast—Amanda, I think—offered to take Mom to the sanctuary with her. It was perfect timing."

Alissa's smile slipped to a frown. "Perfect timing? What's wrong?"

He patted the pocket holding his cell phone. "Business problems. I have to go down to my office in San Luis Obispo tomorrow for a few hours." He raised his brows. "I haven't broken the news to Mom yet."

Her frown changed to what appeared to be disappointment. "I'm sure your mom will do fine. Amanda's staying with us for at least a week of sightseeing and visiting the sanctuary, so I'm sure your mother will be in good company even if you have to go."

Ross studied her face a moment. "How did it go with Fern?"

"Better than I thought." Her eyes turned heavenward. "Praise God, well, really. I think we were open and honest, and we have a place to start with some long-overdue healing."

"You don't look as happy as you should."

The beginning of a grin touched her lips. "Fern's going to work tomorrow for me all day. I hoped to get away and—"

"And join us for some sightseeing and dinner." Personal disappointment sailed over him.

She nodded. "But I can still go along with your mother. She was the one who—"

Ross held up his hand. "I was looking forward to your coming along, too, Alissa. It's not just my mom." Though feeling ill at ease, he charged ahead. "I enjoy your company. I really like you, and that's unusual for me."

The scowl returned. "Unusual? Why?"

"My business is different from yours. You have to be a

people person, so you have skills to be genial and friendly even if you don't want to. My business is business. I deal with produce. Avocados and. . . I don't have to smile at or chat with an avocado."

She chuckled. "I suppose not."

"My life is geared to judging people's honesty and intentions. I'm hesitant with new people, and it carries over into my social life. I'm always looking for an ulterior motive."

"My guests usually don't have those. They're on vacation and want to enjoy the sights."

"That's what I mean. You provide a service. I offer a product. I suppose that's the difference."

She thought for a moment. "What's the problem at your ranch? Anything you can solve by telephone?"

"I tried that." He shook his head. "No go."

She only nodded and lowered her gaze.

The tingle of an idea rose up his back. "If you have the whole day free, why not come with me? I can show you the ranch, and while I'm doing business, you can relax or take a look at the orchard. We could have dinner on the way back. What do you say?"

Her eyes shifted, and a hint of color tinted her cheeks. "I don't know. You're going there for business, and what if it takes longer or you have to stay overnight? Then—"

"That won't happen. The meeting is with one of the companies that distribute our product to the stores. The man won't stay that long. I'm guessing he's harassing more ranches than mine, so he'll be anxious to move on."

"Harassing? Why?"

"Bad weather last spring caused ice damage to some of our crops and slowed the growth of others so we haven't been able to keep up with the guaranteed amount of produce leaving the ranch. But we should have a good harvest from now on, and I have to convince him of that."

She seemed to think it over.

"What do you say about joining me?"

"I'll check with Fern and make sure she has no qualms about my being away from the area for that long. I'll have my cell phone so I can answer most any question. I can't see why—" She paused. "Sorry. I'm thinking aloud."

He slipped his arm around her waist and gave her a friendly hug. "I'm getting used to that."

She grinned, and a deeper flush rose to her cheeks.

⁂

Alissa slipped out of Ross's car, her hair windblown and her cheeks ruddy from the ride. The morning was glorious, and the warm sun had encouraged her to roll down the window and let the autumn air surround her. The air smelled different in San Luis Obispo. A distance from the ocean, the aura of salty water and fish had been replaced by pungent soil and foliage—rich soil that produced grapes, olives, and avocados.

Her interest grew past the fragrance to the rambling buildings in front of her—long buildings with forklifts and long trailers parked nearby, and CAHILL AVOCADOS painted everywhere. From inside she heard rumbling and the echo of voices.

"My office is in here," Ross said, heading toward a door with OFFICE printed on the glass. He held it open, and she stepped inside, noticing the beige walls and dusky brown carpet—so nondescript she would never find a hint of Ross reflected in the decor. He strode through the small waiting room with a couple of tweedy beige chairs and a desk behind a five-foot counter. In this room, one wall was covered by a huge relief map of land—the orchard, she guessed—and two larger prints of avocados filled the other walls, along with smaller photographs of men standing on long ladders, picking the fruit.

"Are these photos old?"

"A few years," he said, eyeing the one she'd been looking at. "They must use machinery to pick them now."

He chuckled. "No. They're still picked by hand. I'll show you in a minute."

A middle-aged woman appeared from a doorway and smiled. "Mr. Cahill. Good morning."

He eyed his watch. "I guess it still is morning, Val." He motioned to Alissa. "This is Alissa Greening. I thought I'd show her what we do here."

"Welcome," Val said.

Alissa smiled. "It's nice to meet you."

Ross's voice broke through the greeting. "You know I have a meeting at one?"

Val nodded. "Yes, Mr. Hershel left the information on your desk, and I've copied what you'll need for the meeting."

"Great. I'll take a look." He took a step forward. "Do you have any coffee?"

"Coffee and tea, if you prefer." She looked at Alissa.

Alissa felt as if she were watching a tennis match. She swiveled her head in one direction then another, seeing Ross in a new light—the owner of a big company. Today in this environment, he seemed more like the Ross she'd met the first night he arrived at the inn.

Ross looked at Alissa. "What's your pleasure?"

"Coffee's fine. . .with cream," she added, speaking to Val.

"Coming up."

Val strode back into the room she'd come from, and Ross opened a door and motioned Alissa to follow.

His office was filled with files, a large desk, three chairs in front of the desk, and a credenza beneath some windows. As she moved closer, photographs on the credenza caught her eye. She spotted Maggie with a gentleman she guessed was Ross's father by the resemblance. "This is your father?"

Ross glanced at the photo and nodded his head. "It was

taken about a year before he died."

Another photo caught her eye, a picture of a younger Ross with an even younger man. His brother, no doubt. "Is this your brother?" She drew the photo closer, looking for a resemblance. She saw it in the shape of his face and the coloring, but otherwise she saw Maggie's features, except for the eyes. Ross had his mother's sparkling eyes that glinted when he laughed yet couldn't cover the sorrow beneath. Losing loved ones could do that.

Ross didn't respond, and she realized he'd sat in his chair behind the desk and was studying the reports the manager had left him.

Instead of bothering him, she moved on and lifted another photo where the sun filtered through the trees at what appeared to be a picnic. They were seated around a picnic table, smiles as wide as the blue sky above the tree line. From the other photos, she recognized Ross's father and mother, his brother, a younger woman, and an older couple. She looked more closely and noticed Ross's hand on the woman's shoulder.

Her heart tripped as she looked at Ross again. He appeared more relaxed in the picture than he did now. His smile was bright, his eyes glinted, and. . .he just looked happier. A sensation rolled through her, as if she had dug too deeply into something she shouldn't see.

"That was a Fourth of July picnic."

Ross's voice penetrated her guilty rumination, and she jumped.

"Sorry," he said, resting his hand on her shoulder. "I didn't mean to scare you."

She managed to laugh. "I guess the photo took me away for a moment. I recognize your parents and brother."

He took the photo from her hand and pointed. "These are my aunt and uncle. My dad's brother. Those were happier days."

"I'm sure they were."

She waited, hoping he'd identify the woman. "Who took the snapshot?"

"My cousin."

Unable to let her curiosity go. "This is another cousin?"

He didn't speak for a moment, and she knew she should have monitored her nosiness.

"No. She was a friend of mine."

"Oh," she said, trying to add an amiable lilt to her voice.

"Audra was my fiancée, actually."

"You didn't marry her?" She held her breath.

"No. She made other decisions, and I'm grateful now." Nostalgia hung in his voice.

"Really?"

"Really. It would have been a disaster. I wasn't ready to marry then."

Then. But was he now?

"Here you go." Val bustled into his office with two mugs of coffee and handed them to her and Ross. "I can make you a sandwich if you'd like."

"Thanks, Val, but I think we'll grab something at the house in a few minutes." He eyed his watch. "Why don't you explain the relief map to Alissa, and I'll be done shortly. I just want to finish reading some of these figures."

"Sure thing." She turned to Alissa. "You can finish your coffee first."

"No, I'll carry it along." She watched Ross sink back into his chair, his gaze glued to the report, and she followed Val into the outer office.

"I noticed this when I came in," she said, standing beside the woman. "I assume this is the orchard."

"It is. We have many acres, and they're divided by types and harvesting cycles."

Alissa noticed a blend of pride and enthusiasm in her voice as she spoke.

"I'm not sure if you know much about avocados."

"Nothing much," Alissa said, "except it's an ingredient of guacamole."

Val chuckled. "We have a wonderful recipe Mr. Cahill loves. I'll have to give you a copy before you leave."

"He told me about it, and I'd love a copy."

Val nodded. "Let me tell you about avocados. California produces about 95 percent of the nation's crop, and most are grown from right here to the Mexican border. The most well-known variety of avocado is Hass, and that's because it grows year-round, unlike the other varieties."

She pointed to the lower section of the map. "All of this area is Hass. As you can see, Mr. Cahill can provide the fruit on a year-round basis. But he decided to expand some of the land going up the mountain, so that area was terraced. And up here"—she pointed to the top of the map—"is where we grow Pinkerton and Zutano avocados."

Alissa studied the huge map, eager to see the property. "Terracing must be a huge undertaking."

"Mr. Cahill owned the land, but making it workable was expensive."

"What do you think?" Ross said, coming toward them.

"I'm impressed." She turned to face him. "I knew nothing about avocados until Val filled me in."

"Let's look at the packinghouse, and then I'll take you on a ride through the orchard."

"Thanks for the coffee," Alissa said, setting her cup on the counter. "And thanks for explaining a little of the business."

"You're welcome," Val said, lifting the cup and carrying it behind the counter.

"I'll be back before one, Val. Chuck Conklin is expected then."

She gave him a wave, and Ross steered Alissa through the doorway.

The sun, warmer here than in Pacific Grove, heated Alissa's arms as she followed Ross across the dusty concrete to the large metal-and-cement-block building. He pulled open a heavy door, and she stepped inside and stopped. In front of her, forklifts moved along the concrete floor, carrying large bins to an area on the other side of the big room where workers guided the bins into what appeared to be a storage room.

She felt Ross close beside her, his aroma mingling with the scent of fruit and dusty air. "What's going on here?"

"Trucks have brought the avocados in from the field in those bins you see, and the forklifts move them into our cold storage, where they'll sit for twenty-four hours to cool from the outdoor heat and to preserve them." He motioned her to follow.

She glanced into the area where they were moving the bins and felt the cooler air from inside. He led her up a set of stairs where she could look below to see what was happening.

"In this area," Ross said, pointing to conveyor belts, "avocados are separated by a grading belt that determines their size. Those workers over there are checking and sorting to make sure the avocados are all the same size. Then they'll be removed from the bins by the belt, which tips the fruit gently so as not to bruise it."

"This is interesting. I had no idea—"

She felt his hand rest against her shoulder. "You had no need to know until now." She liked the sound of his words—"until now." Until now, things had been so different.

"Come with me," he said, grasping her hand and guiding her along.

His hand felt massive around hers, and she could feel his pulse beating against her palm as if their hearts were beating as one. He stopped too soon, releasing her fingers to point.

"Here's where they are brushed and washed then carefully placed in cartons called lugs. And finally"—he grasped her hand again and this time squeezed it—"this area checks the avocados again for quality—size, condition, cleanliness. Then the lug is sealed over there." He drew her along the walkway. "And they're organized here and stacked onto pallets of sixty lugs each."

"Whew. I'll appreciate my avocado more now that I've seen this."

He grinned, slipped his hand from hers, and wrapped his arm around her shoulders. "You've had a quick lesson in avocados."

"Not totally. I'd love to see the orchard."

He drew her against his shoulder. "And you will after lunch. We're heading for the house now."

She'd never been to a ranch before, and her excitement heightened. Alissa felt alive amid the bustle of workers and the clang of machinery. As they descended, she could again see forklifts moving through a wide doorway toward the cooling area. Her heart pulsed with the joy she felt in being here and even more in being with Ross.

six

Ross loved watching the animation in Alissa's face. She'd truly been excited about seeing the packing plant, and he hoped she would enjoy the orchard as much. Although the meeting was here, he almost wished they could make a stop at Paso Robles so he could show her his real headquarters, but for now he believed this was wiser.

He linked his arm in hers as they stepped outside.

"Which way?" she asked.

"We'll take the car." He guided her toward his sedan and opened the passenger door. He saw a questioning look on her face, but he didn't say anything until he slid into the driver's seat. "My house is up that road." He pointed ahead to the blacktop road wending past the trees.

He pulled away, and as he did, Alissa rolled down the window again and rested her arm on the frame. "Are these avocados?" She pointed to the trees along the road.

"No, they're fruit trees—a few for us and a few for the birds."

"The birds?"

"Crabapples and cherries. They love them."

"That's thoughtful," she said. "Do they bother the avocados?"

"Not really. They prefer this fruit."

He noticed her eyeing the peach and orange trees mingled with shade trees as they drove around the bend. His ranch house appeared ahead of them, a solid structure with large rooms, yet so much smaller than his other home. When he'd pulled into the drive, he hurried around to open the door and let her step out. He pulled out his keys and unlocked the side door, and they stepped inside the back hall.

"Go ahead in," he said, slipping off his boots, a habit he'd learned from his mother. "This is the kitchen, as you can see. I have a day lady when I'm here, but otherwise she enjoys the time off. She's not dependent on the money but loves to occupy her time. It works well for me."

Alissa gazed around the room as if taking it all in then wandered through the doorway into the great room, a section of the ranch he'd added with a two-story ceiling with skylights. "This is beautiful, Ross. So airy."

"I enjoy the outdoors, and I felt crushed inside this large room with the low ceiling. It was worth the money, and I added the loft up there." He pointed to his favorite room. "It's my home office. But I have a futon, and some nights, I lie there and look at the stars."

She pivoted, scanning each area of the room, from the fireplace to the seating arranged around the wide windows looking into the orchard then to the loft staircase. "May I go up?"

"You sure can." He followed behind her, her small frame bouncing up each stair, the sunlight glinting in her buttered-toast blond hair.

At the top she let out a cry. "It's wonderful! Is that the orchard?"

He followed and stood behind her at the windows, looking out at the edge of the Hass trees. "Yes, the Hass avocados. That's our largest orchard."

"I know, because they can be picked year round."

He wrapped his arms around her from behind and drew her into his chest. "I'm proud of you. Val must have explained that."

"She did, along with a few other things. I'm a host of knowledge."

Ross pointed toward the rows of trees, aware of her closeness.

He stepped away and suggested they head back down. Not waiting for a response, he led the way.

At the bottom of the stairs, he turned to face her one step up, and Alissa touched his arm. "Thanks so much. It's so nice to see where you live and to understand your work."

Her lips were so close, he could almost feel the softness. Needing to control his emotions, he eased back, resting his hands on her shoulders. "I'm glad you enjoyed it. Are you hungry? I am."

"I could eat something." She took the final step to the floor.

"Let's have a sandwich and then take a ride out there." He wanted to get outside soon and clear his head of the emotions racing through him.

He headed to the kitchen and paused inside the doorway. "Help me be creative." He motioned for her to open the refrigerator, and he stood next to her, studying what was inside.

Alissa chuckled. "Do you have peanut butter?"

"It's that bad, huh?"

"I see some bread in here and lo and behold, an avocado."

He walked away and opened his kitchen pantry. "Do you like tuna salad?"

"With avocado? Yes."

"Then we have lunch." Though he didn't use this house often, he kept canned goods stocked in the pantry. The bread looked fresh enough. He assumed Rosa, his day lady, had come in to clean and left it there. He pulled out a can of albacore, found a can opener in the drawer, and took off the lid.

Alissa had made herself at home. She'd taken out the mayo and had already begun to cut the avocado. "All we need is chips, and this would be gourmet," she said, grinning as she diced the fruit.

His smile broadened as he returned to the cabinet and pulled out an unopened can of chips. "I hope these will work."

"Great. Who could ask for more?"

He loved her lightheartedness. "Can you handle paper plates? I live with them."

"Saves us from dishwashing," she said, wiping the countertop.

Ross watched her separate the tuna flakes, dice up a small onion and add avocado, mix in the mayo, and pile it on the slices of bread she'd placed on the plate. "Sorry. No lettuce."

She waved away his apology. "This will be delicious."

He opened the can of chips and dropped a pile onto each plate. "How about a soda?"

She nodded, and he let her choose then beckoned her to follow. He walked down a short hall and opened the side door to the patio. The umbrella table, lacking the umbrella, looked clean enough, and they settled into the chairs.

Alissa had thought to bring the napkins and handed him one, and with her hand so near, he captured it in his. "I'd like to ask a blessing."

"Please," she said, leaving her fingers in his grasp.

He bowed his head and thanked the Lord for the day, the food, and every blessing, and when he raised his head, Alissa's remained bowed.

When she looked up, she grinned. "I had an addendum."

He felt his eyebrows rise.

"A private addendum," she said with a coy look.

He asked God that her prayer concerned something wonderful about their relationship, because that's where his heart was headed.

When they'd finished their sandwiches and nibbled the chips between swigs of soda, Ross rose and tossed away the paper plates and napkins, dropped the cans into the recyclables, then reached for Alissa's hand. "You want to take a look?" He pointed toward the orchards.

"I can't wait."

He strode around the side to the garage and opened the

door then motioned Alissa inside. He hit the remote and unlocked the doors of his SUV. "This is the only way to travel on a ranch."

She climbed in, and after he backed out to the road, they continued along the asphalt until a cutoff led him into the orchard. With the windows rolled down, the scent of ripe fruit filled the air. Alissa's smile made the sunny day even warmer. Her short hair ruffled in the wind, and she tossed back her head and laughed like a young girl, with a carefree look that melted his heart.

He drove to the top terrace overlooking the lower trees with his home and the packinghouse in the distance. He slowed then stopped and climbed out and walked to the passenger side. "What do you think?" he asked, opening the door.

She slipped out and stood beside him, the trees blocking some of their view. "It's wonderful, Ross. Really. I feel alive and so happy."

"I'm glad." He longed to take her in his arms, but he recalled the earlier emotions he'd felt and stopped himself. Seeing her in his home had made him long for his life to be complete again. Forcing his mind in less romantic directions, he changed the subject. "Too bad I didn't know you sooner. The avocado festival was in Carpinteria the weekend before we came to your place. It's a huge fund-raiser for local nonprofit groups. They have a poster contest and another one for the biggest avocado and another for the best guacamole recipe." He snapped his fingers. "Remind me to give you that guacamole recipe before we leave. It won a couple of years ago."

"I'll remember," she said. "I love the stuff."

He refocused on the orchard. "These are the Zutano variety. They won't blossom and grow again until later in the season, but below we're still picking."

"I noticed. Those ladders are high, plus the long poles."

"Some ladders can extend up to thirty feet, and the poles

can be up to fourteen feet long. Each fruit is picked by hand with a special clipper to assure quality. Bruising ruins the fruit. The nylon bags you saw around their necks hold up to forty pounds. When the bag is full, it's placed in a bin. Those are the large containers you saw coming into the packinghouse."

"Who would think one little avocado took so much work?"

He slipped his arm around her. "Lots of things take work. Think about your inn. It's not easy. You depend on quality service from your cleaning ladies, accuracy and geniality from the person at the reception desk." He felt her wince when he mentioned that job. "The food you prepare, the special amenities that make your inn different from others. Your grounds, the gardens, and gazebo. You have to provide service, charm, and a smile, even when you feel rotten."

She nodded as if she hadn't thought about that. "You make the job sound hard."

"It is, but you enjoy it, and so it's not quite as much work for you." He gestured to the orchard. "This is work and a pain sometimes, but I love it." Work. He glanced at his watch, almost forgetting he'd come to San Luis Obispo for a meeting. "We need to get back. It's getting late."

He grasped Alissa's shoulders and turned her to face him. "May I be honest?"

Her beautiful indigo eyes widened. "Yes."

"This day has been special for me, too." Ross bent down to kiss her cheek. "Thanks for coming with me."

She looked surprised, but she didn't respond for a moment until she grinned. "I loved every minute of it."

Every minute. He hoped that included the kiss.

❧

"And that's it," Ross said, relating the meeting he'd had earlier. "Concessions on both parts. We pay more for two months then back to our original contract, but he guaranteed to give us a discount next year if we exceed our shipping agreement. Give a little; take a little. That's business."

"I'm glad it went well," Alissa said, looking across the bay to Morro Rock, its rugged outcrop soaring above the water. "This is a gorgeous sight."

"It is. I hope you don't mind going back on Highway 1. I know it's nerve-racking, but the scenery is tremendous."

"It is, and I haven't been this way in so long." She thought about her last trip. "I'll enjoy this one more than the last. We took it south on the ocean side of the highway last trip. At least we have the mountain wall going north."

He chuckled. "It does feel safer." He motioned ahead. "I thought we'd look for a place to eat farther up the highway, or would you like to stop here in town?"

"No. I'm not hungry yet. While you were at your meeting, I ate the last few chips in the can. I hope you don't mind."

He chuckled. "You could have eaten anything, and I'd be pleased." He reached over and rested his hand on hers. "You've made my day, Alissa. I'm really glad you came along."

"Me, too," she said, placing her other hand over his and loving the feel of being together.

"I have a place I'll take you then. It's not too far. I think you'll enjoy it."

They settled into silence, and Alissa reminisced about the wonderful day. She'd enjoyed relaxing at Ross's while he went to his meeting. She'd gazed up at the sky, creating cloud pictures, something she never did at home. Afterward Alissa had found a magazine about avocados and skimmed it, learning some new things with the turn of every page. She'd been fascinated by the packinghouse and the orchard and loved seeing Ross's office. Everything seemed beyond what she had anticipated; even the house she thought was rather small for a man with such a lucrative business, she loved despite her previous expectations.

Though Ross had never said he was rich, Alissa knew what

it meant to own a produce farm or orchard in California. It meant living more than well, a life she'd never considered possible for her. The thought gave her an uncomfortable feeling. She loved her inn, and though she would never be rich, she had a good life; she asked God's forgiveness for thinking of material goods when they weren't important in the scheme of things.

"Are you sleeping?"

Ross's voice cut into her thoughts, and she looked up. "No, I'm thinking about the day and what a wonderful time I've had. It was so nice to see where you live and work."

The image of his office credenza filled her mind, and though she'd tried to forget the ex-fiancée's part in Ross's life, she couldn't. "Tell me about Audra. What happened?"

"Audra."

He uttered the name then grew quiet.

Alissa panicked, thinking she might have ruined the perfect day with her question. She wanted to retract it, but obviously it was too late. As she listened to the stillness, except for the hum of the tires on the road, she struggled to find how to cover her error.

"It's not an easy question to answer."

Air shot from her lungs. "I'm sorry I asked, Ross. It's really none of my business."

"It's fine, Alissa. You know, sometimes in life things happen beyond our understanding, but I always think God knows best. At least I've realized that through the years. Like death and loss, we don't know exactly why they happen."

His profile tensed, and Alissa wondered if he were thinking of his father and brother.

Ross's demeanor changed. "Now that I look back, I realize Audra and I weren't meant for each other from the beginning. She was a beautiful woman, and my father thought she would be an asset to our family. She had a knack for stepping into the limelight, for entertaining, and for wearing the right designer—so many things I didn't value, but she did them with style."

Alissa weighed his words. "It was one of those opposites-attract relationships."

"Sort of, yes. But the opposite doesn't sit well in the long run sometimes. While I loved the outdoors, nature, and the work I do, Audra detested ranch life. She tried to adjust and rented a condo in Paso Robles, but she much preferred the more glamorous city life—Santa Barbara, Carmel, and Los Angeles."

"I love the quieter life, I think. I'm not a social butterfly."

He chuckled. "More like a monarch?"

"I wasn't thinking about that," she said, grinning at the metaphor. "I can entertain when I must. I love cooking and showing guests a good time. It's my job."

"You are good at that."

"But I'm not into glitz. Not at all."

"We have that in common," he said, glancing her way.

Her heart skipped as she thought about having things in common with Ross. She loved the life here, the outdoors, nature, but she loved Pacific Grove, too, and her inn. It was her security, and it was what gave her confidence and pride in herself.

"Look at the view."

Alissa looked up. As they rounded a bend in the road, the vista stretched unending with rugged cliffs falling to the ocean where waves lashed against their jagged edges, smoothing them in time and spreading white foam to the shoreline. A mist had begun to hang on the cliffs, an ethereal haze that softened the rocks and spawned an unreal aura that seemed to wrap around the landscape.

"It's unbelievable." She viewed the sun as it lowered toward the horizon, its deepening hues melting into the rolling green water, turning it into shades of amber and coral that rippled with black dimples. "It takes my breath away."

"I know," he said, his voice only a whisper.

Shortly, Ross slowed and turned off Highway 1. They stopped at a traffic light, and soon he guided the car through a split rail fence into a parking lot. "This is it. Cambria Pines Lodge. They have great food and a terrific garden. We can stretch our legs there before we finish the drive."

She slipped from the car and gazed at the old building that looked like someone's rambling house with blue and white trim, nestled among the pines and shrubs a short distance from the dangerous stretch of highway.

The dining room had a quaint look with small print wallpaper and white molding. A stone fireplace stood in the corner, and pine furniture added a fitting look to the homey room. They were seated at a small table by the window, and outside she could see the expansive garden Ross had mentioned, with a winding path that wove past a fountain.

She ordered a tossed salad followed by chicken *piccata* with rice pilaf, and Ross couldn't decide between the grilled fillet with fried onions or the wild salmon. The salmon won out, served with sun-dried tomato, cucumber salsa, and rainbow pasta.

The waitress returned with their iced tea, and when she left, a hush fell over them. Alissa wavered between looking at the scenery outside the window or gazing into Ross's blue eyes. "This is so nice, and I would love to have time to walk outside. Did you see the fountain?"

"They have others. We'll make the time."

"But it gets dark early, and I don't think you want to drive on that highway in the dark."

"I'll be fine. Don't worry." He brushed her cheek. "Now give me your pretty smile and stop worrying about me."

Pretty smile. She hadn't been called pretty by anyone since her mom died. Alissa pulled herself from her thoughts. "You asked earlier about Fern and me."

His face spoke volumes. "It's not my business to ask, but if you ever need a friend to listen, you know I'm here."

"It's one of those long stories like you mentioned with Audra, I guess. Fern and I were never really close. She skittered from one thing to the next. I was quieter. I love to read. Fern liked to argue. I preferred quick resolutions. We were very different. My mom knew that. I had goals early on, and Fern couldn't settle on one thing. She hopped from hobby to hobby then job to job when she was old enough."

"That's what we talked about earlier. Opposites."

"Yes, but it's difficult in families, I think, because we're in a forced-proximity situation."

"True. You can drop a friend who becomes irritating."

She calmed, grateful he seemed to understand.

Ross slid his hand across the terra-cotta–hued tablecloth and rested it over hers. "Has that been your problem with Fern?"

"It worsened when my mother died." She paused, thinking of the anger that had sprouted at that time. "I told you she'd left a small will. We weren't rich, but she had the house and a little savings, mainly from Dad's life insurance and his social security. Mom never worked."

"Some women prefer to be homemakers. My mom, too."

She smiled, sensing more camaraderie with him and Maggie. "The problem arose when my mom left me the house and a smaller portion of her savings, with the rest going to Fern."

"You did tell me that."

"But it got worse. Fern resented me for selling Mom's house to buy the inn. She thought I should keep the family home. Nostalgia, I guess, but I was looking at it from a business standpoint."

"It was wise. The house located on Ocean View Boulevard with the magnificent view will draw in many more guests than a house that's tucked away in the downtown area."

"I know, but I couldn't convince Fern." She felt her hand tighten beneath his, and Alissa tried to relax. "The worst part was—and I don't know if it was spite or just her nature—Fern wasted her money. She bought an expensive car and a complete new wardrobe. She met a man who convinced her to loan him money for this great business deal, and then he vanished. Fern didn't have that much to begin with so she ended up with little left, and I loathed the situation."

"I can understand how bad you must have felt."

She looked into his eyes. "I didn't just feel bad. I was bitter. I saw my mom's skimping and saving and then how Fern tossed her gift away. I couldn't forgive her for that, and I've held it against her all this time."

Ross didn't say anything for a few minutes. His gaze left her to look out the window. Finally he turned back. "It really wasn't up to you how Fern spent or wasted her money. Do you realize that now?"

"I do, but I still begrudge her."

"Then you have to work on that, I guess." His face darkened as the words left him.

Alissa longed to know what thought had shadowed his face. "I'm hoping to do that. I think we have a start. When we talked, I told her the truth, and I think just getting it out in the open helped both of us. She resented my getting the house and selling it. We'd both let each other down."

Ross nodded. "It's easy, isn't it, to let people down. I've done that myself, Alissa, and it's hard to forgive ourselves." He quieted a moment before continuing. "I think that's often the problem. We can forgive others, but we can't forgive ourselves."

Alissa's pulse skipped a beat. Was that it? As the idea settled into her mind, she realized how close to the truth Ross had come. The problem was forgiving herself, and now she had a new place to start. "Thank you."

"Thank me? For what?"

"For being you."

Though her words were interrupted by the waitress, she needed Ross to know how important he'd become in her life. He'd made a difference, such a difference that she didn't know what she would do without him.

seven

Heavy floral fragrances mingled with warm earth and the distant scent of the ocean. The muted sun hid beyond the ancient pines and cottages, leaving a shadowed walk, and around the bend, Alissa came upon the trickling water of a fountain. As they continued, she read the signs marking the gardens—herbs, succulents, and organic produce served in the lodge's kitchen.

Alissa stopped beside a flower garden, admiring the clusters of colorful blossoms, almost as bright as her life had become since she'd met Ross. "I wish I had a camera."

"I'd love to take your picture here," Ross said, his eyes searching her face. "You look more relaxed and more beautiful than you have since I met you."

Heat rose up her neck. "It's the flush on my cheeks. You're making me blush."

"Then you should blush all the time."

Her pulse skittered along her limbs and fluttered in her temples. Sensations she'd never felt before washed over her—contentment, comfort, joy, untold happiness—but as reality struck her, she feared being hurt. "You're silly."

"I'm being honest."

He slipped his hand into hers, and she knew her pulse pounded against his palm. Alissa had no idea how to control the emotion she felt. She loved it and hated it because it made her feel out of control.

"You shouldn't talk like this," she said, hearing the breathless sound of her voice.

"Why?"

"Because it sounds romantic, and it can't be."

"I don't understand, Alissa."

"First, we barely know each other, and second, our worlds are in different places."

Ross stopped beside a towering tree and drew her toward him so they stood face-to-face in the dappled sunlight. He lifted her hand and pressed it against his chest. "Can you feel this?"

She closed her eyes, and beneath her palm, his heart thumped in a steady rhythm. "I can feel your heartbeat."

"As sure as my heart is beating, you have the same certainty of how much I care about you. I know we've only known each other a short time, but can we question how the Lord works? I didn't want to go to Pacific Grove. I work long hours, and I'm antsy when I'm home without my work. I came here for my mother, as you know, but things have changed. Now I sense God guiding me in a direction I never thought possible."

Alissa lowered her gaze, fearing she would be entrapped by his beautiful eyes. "I'm not saying we haven't connected. I'd be lying if I did. I love your company. I think your mother is a wonderful woman. I hate thinking of your leaving because I know life will slip back into its usual rut. But—"

"Life doesn't have to be a rut, Alissa. I'm not saying we're ready for commitment, and yes, we have things to learn, but I want time to get to know you better. I don't want to go back home and never see you again."

Tears pooled in her eyes. "I don't want that either."

"Then let's agree we won't let go of this great beginning."

A ragged breath fluttered from her. "I'd like to get to know you better. I really would."

He pulled her into his arms, and through her tear-filled eyes, she studied his face and knew he meant every word. As her gaze met his, she watched his lips lower to hers, a tender kiss that was there and gone in a heartbeat, but one she would remember forever.

She buried her head against his chest, thinking of his home and work in San Luis Obispo and hers in Pacific Grove—a hundred miles away. How could two hardworking people get to know each other with those circumstances?

Not wanting to think about the impossible, she straightened, and he slipped his arm around her waist and led her back toward the restaurant from a different direction. A few moments later she faltered, seeing a wishing well surrounded by another glorious flower bed. As they neared, Ross paused while her gaze shifted from the fairy-tale wishing well to his face.

"I don't believe in wishing wells, do you?"

She managed a smile. "No."

He touched her hand. "We both believe in prayer."

Her pulse did a jig. "Yes."

"Then let's both pray, Alissa, that the Lord guides us in the path He has planned for us."

"And that we can hear His wisdom, whatever it may be."

Ross squeezed her hand. "Amen." He pulled a coin from his pocket and tossed it into the well. "God's power is all we need, but tossing in a coin is still fun."

"It's like blowing out birthday candles. No matter what we do, God's in charge."

He sent her a gentle smile that lifted her beyond her doubts. *Thank You, Lord,* she thought, grasping his hand as they headed back to the car.

❧

Ross supported his mother's arm as they followed the guide through the Monarch Butterfly Sanctuary. Since he'd last visited the site, the butterflies had multiplied, and today they hung in heavy clusters on the pine and eucalyptus trees like dried leaves caught among the green branches. Whether he was a fan of butterflies or not, the image was an amazing sight, and it would only have been better if Alissa had been able to join them.

They paused as the young woman continued with her spiel.

"As you know, the monarchs travel as far as two thousand miles, but you may not know they can cover a hundred miles a day at a height of up to ten thousand feet. Picture these fragile creatures being driven by instinct back to the same place their ancestors have come for years."

Driven by instinct. Ross understood that feeling. God had created man and woman so they didn't have to live alone and so they could procreate and populate the earth. He'd given up on that idea years ago when his relationship with Audra had crumbled like dried clay. It left a mess with nothing good coming out of it. He'd never wanted to have that happen again, and every relationship he'd encountered tended to leave him with the dried-clay feeling. But Alissa. . . She was different.

The guide's voice surged back into his consciousness. "Let's head this way." The woman beckoned them to follow and continued her talk. "When you think about the short life of a butterfly, you will realize no butterflies here today were here last year. They are guided totally by a genic message that triggers them to follow the same route as their ancestors to arrive here the same time each year. Some scientists think they may rely on the earth's magnetic field and the position of the sun, but some believe it's a gift."

"A God-given gift," his mother whispered.

Ross agreed. The Lord had ways to guide His creatures, from the most fragile butterfly to a husky forty-five-year-old like Ross Cahill, and Ross sensed that God had tucked a message in his heart.

"This way," the guide said. "Be careful—the stone walkway is rough here."

His mother paused and pointed down a connecting path. "Let's sit there for a minute."

Ross veered her toward the seat he saw in the distance beneath a large pine. As he neared, he eyed the amazing bench in the shape of a butterfly, its back the upper wings and its legs the lower wings with a cross piece that served as a seat. His mother sat, but Ross eyed the delicate sculpture and decided not to chance it.

"Are you enjoying yourself?"

"It's amazing, Mom. Hard to believe those little things make their way here every year."

"But can you blame them?" She grinned. "It is beautiful."

"It's very interesting, and since it's their first time here, how do they know the way?"

"God created the little beings to know. Sometimes we know things, too. It's in our hearts without facts or even common sense."

Her words settled in his thoughts, and as she spoke, an orange and black monarch fluttered past, settled on the pine a moment, then spread its wings and flew off. Yesterday he'd seen Alissa spread her wings. Each day she grew more and more a part of his life until—

"How was your day yesterday?"

His mother's voice intruded on his thoughts. He lowered his gaze. "Nice. Alissa enjoyed the packinghouse, and I took her for a ride into the orchard."

"You got back very late."

He tried not to smile. His mother's grilling made him feel like a teenager again. "We stopped for dinner in Cambria."

"Cambria?" Her eyes widened. "You came back on Highway 1?"

"Yes."

"Ross, you know that's a treacherous highway at night. You should never—"

"Mom, I drove it, so I know. I was careful. We decided to walk through the Cambria Pines Lodge gardens, and that took longer than I thought, so it was dusk when we left. I'm home, and I'm safe."

"Yes, but it was pitch-dark when you drove through Big Sur, right?"

"Right." No sense in arguing. He would bow to her lecture, and she was correct. It had been a dumb thing to do, and Alissa had been nervous, too; the kiss in the garden had been wonderful, though, so he didn't regret the stop.

"Please promise me you'll use your head next time."

He leaned over and kissed her cheek. "I promise."

"Thank you." She tilted her head upward and grinned. "You like Alissa."

"She's a very nice woman."

"I know that. She's wonderful, but that's not what I mean."

He drew in a lengthy breath and shook his head. "No. I'm not going there."

She rose and gave him one of her "mother's always right" looks then started down the path. "Never mind. I already figured it out. I've never seen you so attentive to a woman. Not even Audra."

Her words struck him as he stood to follow her. He'd blamed Audra for walking away from him, but perhaps he'd walked away from her emotionally. Her leaving had been a blessing. He'd realized that long ago. Marriage was forever, and his relationship with Audra wouldn't have lasted.

"Look." She pointed ahead.

He jerked from his thoughts and saw his mother hurrying ahead to view an astonishing cluster of monarchs in a nearby tree, their wings open wide, fluttering like petals of orange flowers in a breeze. As he watched her, Ross saw his mother stumble. He darted forward, feeling helpless as she lurched forward, reeling to catch her balance before she collapsed to the ground against a boulder along the path.

"Mom, are you okay?"

Her moan filled his ears, and when he looked at her face, he knew she wasn't okay at all. His heart thundering, he knelt beside her. "Don't move, Mom." He rested his hand against her arm to keep her from shifting. "Where does it hurt?"

She didn't answer for a moment. "My upper leg. Maybe my hip."

The pain in her eyes cued him. Her injury was worse than he wanted to think. "Let me run back, Mom, and get help. Please don't move."

The unnecessary request struck him. Horrendous pain registered on her face. He gave her a pat while fear gripped him. Ross pulled out his cell and dialed 911, praying the fall wasn't as bad as he knew it was.

❧

Alissa checked the time again. Ross and Maggie had left early, and she'd thought they'd be back in the afternoon. She'd made more lemon bars, and since they hadn't arrived, she kept a plateful in the kitchen so Ross would be sure to get some.

Trying to distract herself, she checked the buffet one more time then wandered into the sitting room where a husband and wife were relaxing. "How was your day?"

"Wonderful," the woman said. "We spent a couple of hours at the sanctuary, and then we went to the wharf for lunch."

"I'll do anything to keep her from shopping," the husband said and chuckled.

"Most husbands don't like—" The telephone jarred her thought. Alissa gave them an apologetic shrug and turned toward the call. "Butterfly Trees Inn. May I help you?"

"Alissa, this is Ross."

Hairs prickled on her neck at the sound of his tense voice. "What's wrong?"

"Mom fell at the sanctuary."

"Fell?" Her pulse escalated. "Is she hurt?"

"We're in the emergency at Community Hospital of the Monterey Peninsula."

"Emergency?" Her mind filled with questions. "What did the doctors say?"

"Probably surgery. They think it's her hip, but they needed to do X-rays before they know how bad. I'm in the waiting room."

Surgery. Hip. She turned her back on the couple seated nearby, not wanting them to see the tears forming in her eyes. "What can I do?" She knew what she wanted to do. Be with him.

"Pray. That's what I'm doing."

"I'm sending up prayers now, Ross. Was she conscious?"

"Yes, but in a lot of pain. Mom didn't know which hurt worse—her hip or her leg."

Alissa grimaced. "How did it happen?"

"We stopped so she could sit on a bench while the docent went on ahead with the group, and then when we started again, she saw a beautiful cluster of monarchs nearby and dashed off but apparently tripped over a rock or something. She was in a lot of pain, and I called 911. It broke my heart to see Mom in so much pain. She's always so healthy and—"

"Healthy's the key. If she's in good health, then we can hope she'll heal quickly if anything's broken." If Alissa had to choose a break, she'd wish for a broken leg. They healed more quickly. She didn't even want to think of a hip fracture. "When did it happen?"

"Around eleven thirty. We were about ready to leave for lunch, and she wanted to go to the museum afterward."

"You must be miserable, Ross. Keep me posted, okay?"

"I'll call you as soon as I hear something. I'd better let you go, but I thought you'd want to know."

"I'm pleased you called. I was beginning to wonder, and know that I'm praying."

"Thanks. I'll keep you informed."

She heard a click ending their conversation, and she struggled to keep the sadness from her face as she turned back to the guests. "Enjoy the treats." She gave them a smile and headed back into the kitchen.

Once she was through the door, tears rolled down her cheeks. Maggie had become a dear friend, almost like a mother figure, and Alissa couldn't bear to think of her in pain. She paced the kitchen, trying to think of what to do. She eyed the clock again. Surgery would take so long if Maggie needed it, and Ross was alone.

Alissa knew what she had to do—what she wanted to do. She grasped the kitchen phone and punched MEMORY ONE. She clenched her lips together, praying Fern would answer, and when she did, Alissa got herself under control.

"Is there any way you could come over and work tonight?"

"Another date?"

Alissa weighed the sound of the words, trying to decipher between envy, sarcasm, or acceptance. She chose the latter. "Wish it were. Maggie—you remember Ross's mother—fell at the butterfly sanctuary, and she's in emergency in Monterey."

"I'm sorry. Is it serious?"

"Ross is waiting to hear. They took her up for X-rays. I guess it's her hip. I'm praying it's not a break."

"You want to go up there?"

"If you can come. I'm miserable here, knowing he's alone and wondering what's happening."

"I can be there in a few minutes. Get ready."

"Thanks, Fern. This means so much to me."

"That's nice to hear, Alissa. I'll be there in a flash."

Alissa hung up the receiver with Fern's words ringing in her ears. *That's nice to hear.* She thought back, trying to remember how many times she'd never properly thanked Fern or ever said how much her help meant. People wanted to know they were doing a good job.

eight

Ross took a sip of the strong coffee and closed his eyes. *Surgery.* He hadn't expected it. Since his mother's fall, he'd prayed fervently; the Lord had His reasons, though, and Ross couldn't fight the Lord. Christians often asked, Why me? Why did this happen to so and so? They were such good people. Why a child? Why this? Why that? Questions fell like raindrops, but the answers were a drought. God knew the full scheme of things. All things had a purpose, and Ross would know the answer only when it didn't matter anymore because he'd be with God.

A stream of air whispered from his lips. After Dr. Louden from the ER had let him know it was a hip fracture, he'd allowed him to visit his mother for a moment. The look on his mother's face hung in his mind.

"How do you feel, Mom?" he'd asked.

"Not like jogging."

Her witty response had taken him by surprise. "I don't suppose. You need to have surgery. You know that."

Her eyes searched his. "I know. What I did was so careless. . . and dumb."

"You were excited, Mom. Those monarchs with their wings open looked like flowers."

"They did, and I didn't get a photograph."

He wanted to tell her she'd get there another day, but he stopped himself. She'd know he was only trying to cover his fear. "Maybe I can get one for you."

"Would you?"

Her voice sounded so plaintive that his voice caught in his throat. "I'd do anything for you." He leaned over and kissed her cheek. "Mom, I'll see you when you're out of surgery, and I'm praying."

Her eyes fluttered, and he realized she'd had a shot to make her drowsy. She licked her lips and tried to speak. "Pray. . . ."

"I am, Mom." He backed out of the room and returned to the waiting room where he'd paced. He looked at a magazine. He paced some more. He opened his cell to call Alissa again but had no new information, so he slipped the phone back into his pocket.

Now with the time still dragging, Ross eyed the wall clock and rose again, searching for a new magazine. His stomach growled. He and his mother had missed lunch. *Lunch*. With this sad event, his mom would miss much more than lunch. A few chairs over, he spotted a *Time* magazine and grasped it then turned toward his seat and came to a dead stop. "Alissa."

She walked toward him, her arms open in greeting, and he welcomed her embrace, holding her close and cherishing the feeling of her slender frame in his arms.

"How is she?"

"She's still in surgery."

"Still?"

"It's a hip fracture, but they can't tell the severity until they really take a look."

"I'm so sorry about this. Your mom's such a delight and so excited about her vacation."

"Let's sit." He pointed to the chair beside his, dropped the magazine on the table, and sank into the cushion. "How did you get here?"

"Car."

He gave her a feeble grin. "I know that. I mean, how did you arrange it? You have—"

"Fern came over."

"That was nice of her."

"She wanted me to be with you."

"Really?" Pleased at the changed relationship between Fern and Alissa, he felt his eyebrows rise.

"You know, Ross, I realized today that I rarely tell Fern she's done a good job. I say thanks, but it's one of those perfunctory ones you say to a stranger at the supermarket who lifts the laundry soap off a top shelf for you or holds open a door. I've had expectations, and when she didn't meet them, I told her so; otherwise I said little."

He searched her face a moment, wanting to respond with something meaningful. "Sometimes it takes a tragedy to realize where we went wrong. It's never too late to say thanks and mean it or give her a compliment when she deserves one."

Alissa nodded, her expression thoughtful. "It hit me today that she did a great job while I was gone with you yesterday. She made three reservations. I could read them, and she was very explicit—two people, one room—so I knew she'd marked it accurately."

Her comment triggered a new thought. "She was the one who made my reservation, I suppose."

"She was, and I let her know about it."

"I hope you said something to her yesterday after our talk."

"I did, but not enough. I told her she was doing a good job and how much I appreciated it." She shifted on her hip to face him more directly. "You know what she did? She baked two kinds of cookies and made double batches so we could freeze some. They'll taste fine and save me from baking every day. I've always done that for my guests, except once during an emergency when Fern—" She waved her words away.

"Sounds as if Fern had an innovative idea."

"She did. Why hadn't I thought of doing that? I'm such a stickler for fresh this and that. Cookies frozen right after they cool are still fresh if you use them within the month."

"You don't have to convince me." His stomach growled with the talk of food.

She grinned. "I forgot." She lifted her shoulder bag and pulled out a sack. "I made you a ham and cheese sandwich. I figured you'd missed lunch, and you'll find two lemon bars inside the bag, too."

He held the sack in his hands, emotion knotting in his chest. "Thanks so much. I am hungry, and I hate to leave, even to go to the cafeteria."

"I'd feel the same." She motioned to the food. "Go ahead. Eat. I had lunch."

Ross opened the lunch bag and pulled out the sandwich she'd placed on one of the inn's lacy-looking lilac paper plates. He pulled off the plastic wrap and took a bite. She'd added lettuce and some kind of spicy mayo he'd never had. "It's delicious. What's the sauce?"

"Mayo with chipotle seasoning. It adds a little tang."

"It's great." He took another bite, watching her eyes follow his every move as he chewed and swallowed. "You're a wonderful woman, Alissa."

"Anyone would bring you a sandwich."

"I wouldn't say that, but this has nothing to do with the food, although I appreciate it more than I can say." He reached over and brushed the back of his fingers against her cheek. "I'm talking about you."

She lowered her eyes then drew in a breath. "Thank you."

"Even my mom agrees."

She scooted forward to the edge of the chair. "You were talking about me to your mom?"

"She started it." He slipped his hand over hers.

"Maggie did?"

He nodded. "She asked me if I liked you."

"I hope you said yes."

"That wasn't what she meant. She meant do I *like* you."

Alissa chuckled. "Aha. There's a difference, I suppose."

He noted color rising in her cheeks. "You know there is."

Ross couldn't believe he was going in this direction, but it was a wonderful distraction.

"And what did you say?"

"I'm not going there."

A frown swallowed her sweet grin. "Why not?"

"That's what I said to her."

She thought that over awhile then laughed. "I see."

The last bite of sandwich tasted as good as the first, and Ross wadded the plastic wrap and slipped it into the bag before pulling out the lemon bars—bars she'd made for him, and he knew it.

"Would you like something to drink?" he asked, rising to get a fresh coffee.

"No, I brought a bottle of water." She reached into her bag and pulled out the drink.

"What else do you keep inside that thing?"

"I'm not going there either."

For the first time that day, Ross laughed, and it felt great. He ambled to the coffeemaker, poured a fresh cup, and returned, anxious to tackle the lemon bars. But before he did, he heard his name. He spotted the surgeon and motioned for Alissa to follow.

"Mr. Cahill, your mother has a broken hip, but she was very lucky. We were able to put in a pin that will hold it in place without the added complications of a metal plate. Her recovery will be quicker, although I need to warn you—she'll need extensive therapy and be unable to be alone for a couple of months. We recommend a nursing home, and after she's released, she'll still need home care."

His words spun in Ross's head. *Pin. Extensive therapy. Unable to be alone. Months. Home care.* Overwhelmed by the news, he stood in shock, not able to remember questions he wanted to ask. "Can I see her?"

"It'll be awhile. She's in recovery, but once she's awake, the nurse will call you in."

"About how long?"

"Another hour maybe." He stepped back. "Your mother is in excellent health. That makes a big difference. We hope she'll be able to get back to most of her activities in eight months to a year."

The surgeon turned and walked away while Ross stood with his mouth hanging open and watched him go.

Alissa gave his arm a squeeze. "He said your mom was lucky, but you know what?"

"What?"

She smiled. "I say she was blessed. She'll be fine, Ross. Your mom isn't a quitter. She'll fly through therapy and be walking in no time."

"I hope so."

She put the palms of her hands on his cheeks. "You know so."

His heart beat so fast that he could only nod.

❧

Alissa watched the door throughout the next evening. It was nearly nine o'clock when Ross came in looking tired and miserable. "How is she tonight?"

"Angry that they're trying to get her up already."

"It's important."

"I know, and she does, too. But she's on pain medication, and she's not herself." He leaned against the registration desk. "Actually, they had her walking twice today."

"That's wonderful. When will they move her?"

"In a couple of days. They want to keep an eye on her vital signs. This is a bad time for blood clots and pneumonia. I feel better with her being at Community Hospital."

"But she'll be in good care in a nursing home."

"I suppose." He looked away as if his mind were still at the hospital.

Alissa touched his arm. "Are you hungry?"

"I grabbed something in the cafeteria at four when they took her in for therapy. I'm okay."

She beckoned him into the kitchen. "Have something to drink." She motioned for him to sit at the table then brought out a can of cola and popped the lid. "Here." She crossed the room and brought back a small plate of lemon squares. "What about your work?"

"I thought about that. I'll have to go down for a day or two and make arrangements. I hope Mom understands."

"She will, and I'll take your place. I know that's not quite the same, but I'll make sure I get there each day to visit her."

He gave her a tender smile. "You're too good to me."

"Never." His look sent her heart on a surfer's ride on the crest of a wave.

"I know everything will work out. It's just making plans. Obviously I hadn't expected this to happen, and being away two weeks was bad enough, but now. . ."

He fell silent, and she didn't interrupt the quiet.

Finally Ross gave a one-shoulder shrug followed by a faint grin. "I'll manage."

"Any ideas what you'll do about your mom's care?"

He drew in a lengthy breath. "I don't know. She can't ride home in a car. I'll either have to get an ambulance to take her back home for her therapy, or I suppose I could let her stay here and get through her therapy at least. I'll hire someone to stay with her when she's home."

"I've been thinking." She weighed the words before releasing them. "She can stay with me."

Ross scowled, his eyes questioning.

"I can spare a room. Gratis, naturally. Things slow down this time of year once the weather turns colder, and you know I'm here all day or Fern is. If we're both gone, which is rare, I have competent help that will fill in."

"I couldn't do that."

"Why not?"

"It's a huge responsibility. Why would you want to take on that job?"

Her heart gave her the answer. "Because I think a lot of your mom, and you need help. I know you can't stay here. You have to go back to work, and if I do this, it will help you."

He ran his fingers through his hair. "You're unbelievable."

She didn't think so. It's what people were supposed to do—treat others as they would like to be treated—but this was different. She'd be doing it for two people she'd grown to. . .what? *Like? Care about? Love?* Alissa felt breathless as the questions rattled in her mind. Love was impossible. No one could fall in love in only a few days. That was what fairy tales were made of, or those soap operas. Not real life.

Ross took a swig of the drink, set it down, then fingered the plastic wrap and pulled out a lemon bar. He took a bite, his thoughts seeming miles away. "I'll have to give all of this some thought. I don't have the answers now."

She didn't want to push, so she backed off. He needed time to let things sink in, and she had all the time in the world. "I had a good talk with Fern last night."

He turned toward her as if grateful she'd changed the subject. "Good. Any outcomes?"

"We hugged. I told her I noticed how she'd made every effort to clarify the registration, and I thanked her again for the cookies. She looked shocked when I told her what a great idea it was to bake a double batch—that I'd never thought about it."

"And that surprised her, I suppose."

"I think it did. She said she thought I wouldn't consider them fresh enough, but she did it because she figured I could use a rest."

"How true. We all need a rest." He took a final drink of the soda and set down the can then turned and drew her into his arms.

"I had some thoughts myself, Alissa. Yesterday I realized Audra wasn't the only one at fault in our relationship. I know it always takes two, but I really believed she had been the biggest problem. But something my mother said yesterday made me think."

Alissa held her breath, waiting to hear what it had been, but when Ross said nothing more, she released the air, disappointed. "Mothers can be very wise."

He nodded then tilted her head upward. "Mom said she'd never seen me so attentive to a woman as I am to you. Not even Audra."

A soft gasp slipped from Alissa's throat. "Ross."

"And it's true. You're on my mind all the time, and in a good way. I even find myself smiling when I think of something you said or did."

Watch your heart, Alissa. Warnings shot through her. She knew one day Ross would need to go home, to live his life in San Luis Obispo, and she would live in Pacific Grove. They both had their businesses, their careers, their identities. Their friendship could lead nowhere.

"Did I upset you?"

His voice sounded sad, and it broke her heart. "No. I'm overwhelmed, I guess. I think of you, too, but I said it before. We live in different worlds, Ross, and—"

His mouth covered hers and ended her sentence. The gentle kiss lingered a moment; then he eased back as his gaze captured hers. "Don't think why this can't work, Alissa. Think how it can work. Let's not limit God's power. Do you know what I was thinking today?"

She shook her head.

"Besides you, the one thing that would keep me here is my mother. Do you see how it worked out?"

His comment startled her. "You think God broke your mother's hip to keep you here in Pacific Grove?"

"Not exactly, but if it had to happen, it happened here, here where someone loves her enough to offer to care for her, someone who's only known her for a few days, someone with a heart that's as big as the sky."

Alissa gazed at him, overcome by what he'd said, but she agreed. If Maggie had to have a fall, she thanked the Lord she was there to help.

❧

"You're doing so well," Alissa said, inching her way along the hospital corridor with Maggie at her side clinging to her walker.

"I feel like a turtle."

"But a perky turtle." She patted Maggie's arm. "I know how disappointed you are, but you looked forward to being in Pacific Grove, and now you'll be here even longer than you expected."

Maggie chuckled for the first time since her injury, and Alissa loved the sound.

"Let me tell you a secret," Alissa said, feigning a conspiracy as she spoke in a hushed voice. "I'm trying to convince Ross to let you stay here for a while once you're out of the nursing home."

"Stay here?" A scowl dislodged her smile.

"With me at the inn."

Maggie's head drew back as if she didn't quite believe what she'd heard. "With you? But you don't want all that extra work."

Alissa chuckled. "You sound like Ross." She slipped her arm around Maggie's shoulders. "Our workload slows down in the winter. We have only a few guests, and either I'm there or Fern is. You're in a room on the first floor. It works out so well, rather than having you go back and sit at Ross's with a stranger caring for you."

Maggie seemed to think about it a moment. "I'd like that

better, but I couldn't let you do that for free. I'd want to pay you."

"No. Absolutely not."

"For the room at least."

"Not at my prices." She chuckled at Maggie's expression.

"You make me laugh, Alissa, and it feels good." She tilted her head toward her room. "Could we sit for a while?"

Alissa eyed her watch. They'd been walking for about six minutes, and that seemed pretty good to Alissa. She nodded and helped Maggie into a comfortable chair rather than her bed. Alissa tilted up the footrest then sank into another chair nearby.

"I'm being moved tomorrow," Maggie said after a long silence.

"I know, but I think you'll like it better. It's more like a hotel than a hospital. You'll have other people going through therapy for company. It'll be different."

"I keep telling myself that."

"The doctors think you're doing amazingly well."

"That's what they say." She wiggled in the chair as if trying to get comfortable.

Alissa rose and pulled a pillow from her bed. "Do you want this under your leg or behind your back?"

"My back, I think."

She settled the pillow there then returned to her chair. "Ross is coming back from Paso Robles today."

"He called me this morning." Maggie raised her eyes to the wall clock. "He should be here soon."

Alissa glanced at the time. "Any minute."

She looked more comfortable with the pillow, but Alissa had been noticing something in her eyes and wondered what was going on in Maggie's mind. She looked as if she had something she needed to talk about, but Alissa didn't know how to drag it from her.

Maggie finally looked her way. "What are you and Ross going to do?"

"To do?"

"About your relationship."

The desire to deny or to avoid responding pressed against Alissa's mind. "I know you're Ross's mother so you're concerned about him, but to be honest, Maggie, I don't know."

"He cares about you very much."

"And I care about him, but—"

Neither spoke for a moment until Maggie broke the silence. "It's the *but* that worries me."

"It worries me, too. I keep pinching myself to make sure this is real. It happened so fast, a connection so amazing it seems unreal."

"That's how God works, Alissa. Don't doubt Him."

"I keep telling myself that."

"You keep telling yourself what?"

Ross's voice flew from the doorway, startling Alissa and making her wonder if he'd heard the discussion.

"How are you, Mom?" He strode across the room and kissed her cheek, bringing with him the fresh scent of outdoors clinging to his clothing. He slipped off his lightweight denim jacket, revealing a burgundy knit shirt beneath.

He turned. "Alissa."

She nodded.

Maggie's voice halted the uncomfortable silence. "Go ahead and kiss the girl, Ross. What's wrong with you?"

Ross's eyes widened, and he chuckled. "Thanks, Mom."

He leaned down and kissed Alissa's cheek, whispering, "More later."

As he headed back to Maggie, he veered off and dug a packet from his jacket pocket. "Here you go, Mom. This is to prove I keep my promises."

"What's this?" She reached out and took what looked to Alissa like a photo sleeve.

Maggie drew the folder from the sleeve and pulled out

the photos as her eyes brightened. "Ross, these are beautiful. Come look, Alissa."

Alissa shifted to her side and gazed at the wonderful shots of the monarchs clinging in huge clumps to the green branches. "They're gorgeous. When did you take these?"

"On the way here." He gave Alissa a wink. "I promised Mom. She has a digital camera, so I stopped by the pharmacy up the road and printed them right there. They're hot off the press."

Maggie hadn't taken her eyes from the pictures. "I love these." She held them against her chest.

"I love you, Mom." He took the photographs from her hand, slid them back into the folder, and set it on her bedside table. "So how are you?"

"Great. Alissa and I just came back from a walk."

"Good for you." He grinned at Alissa. "Thanks. I owe you a good dinner or—"

She shook her finger at him. "You owe me nothing. I'd do anything for this lady."

Maggie smiled. "Did you hear that?"

"Miss Greening, you're getting me into trouble."

His voice sounded playful, and it dawned on Alissa he'd come back from the ranch in a good mood.

"How did it go?"

Ross sat on the edge of the bed. "I have a reprieve. Everything's set for a couple of weeks more; then I'll have to go back. I brought my trusty laptop with me. That'll help, and naturally I have my cell for emergencies. But Hersh is capable, and so is Diaz."

Diaz. She'd never heard Ross mention him, but that shouldn't be a surprise. He had a multitude of employees.

She listened while Maggie and Ross talked about her move the next day, but her mind clung to her discussion with Maggie. She sensed Maggie liked her and accepted her friendship with Ross. She'd even encouraged a kiss, so why would she doubt it? But she knew a mother wanted to protect her son, and Alissa wanted to protect herself. The more she thought about their relationship, the more impossible it seemed, and she still sensed that Ross had something on his mind that troubled him. Though he tried to hide it, his eyes reflected a kind of inner struggle. Was it guilt or sadness or remorse?

She might never know.

nine

Ross held open the passenger door as Alissa scooted out and headed inside. Though the worship service had lifted her spirit, she'd noticed that same distant look in Ross's eyes and knew he still struggled with whatever had been bothering him since they'd met.

"I think I'll drive over to the nursing home and spend some time with Mom, but I want to talk with you a moment first if you can spare the time."

Alissa's gaze searched his. "Sure." She looked toward the inn and noticed the curtain shift back. Though she knew Fern had heard them arrive, she hoped her sister would give them a minute alone. She turned and headed to the gazebo, hoping Ross would finally tell her whatever it was that bothered him, but in her heart, she feared the talk had to do with them—that he might give her an ultimatum.

He motioned her toward a bench then sat beside her.

"I understand, Ross," she said before he could say anything. "I've given it a lot of thought."

Ross gave her a curious look. "Thought about what?"

"About us. Isn't that what you want to talk about?"

He looked as if he wanted to grin, but stress muted it. "No, but maybe we should talk about that, too."

He'd thrown her. "I just expected—"

"I'm not giving up on us, Alissa. In fact, our relationship is what brought on the need to talk with you."

Her chest tightened with the seriousness of his voice. "I'll be quiet and listen."

He covered her hand and drew it into his. "Can you take off

tomorrow? I'd like to take you south again. I'll talk with Mom today. She's already made lots of friends at the nursing home, and so I'm comfortable with leaving her alone for the day. If we get back early enough, I can still drop by and see her."

"I thought you'd taken care of everything for a couple of weeks." She searched his face, wanting to understand what was wrong.

"Not everything. I'd like you to go with me if you can. . . and if not, there's no sense in my going."

He'd confused her. "What's this about?"

"I want to show you. Think you can make arrangements?"

Faltering between wanting to learn what it was about and not wanting to be hurt, Alissa couldn't find her voice.

Ross rose. "Think about it, okay? I need to head over and see my mother." His voice flooded with disappointment.

She reached for him and caught his arm. "Ross, I'll check with Fern. If not tomorrow, will another day work? I don't know her schedule."

"Whatever you can arrange. I just decided to do this, and I wanted to get it. . .get to it."

Get it over with. That's what he'd started to say.

Alissa didn't like surprises, and she felt certain this was one she didn't want at all. Yet Ross needed to deal with something, and she seemed a part of it.

He turned away and headed for his car without another word.

"I'll see you when you get back."

He lifted his hand to let her know he heard, but he didn't turn around. The old attitude she'd disliked when Ross arrived had made its appearance again.

What could be so important? Her pulse raced, her mind conjuring up horrendous possibilities.

❧

Ross tried to draw Alissa out, but she'd been quiet since he asked her yesterday to go with him to his office. He understood he'd been rather cryptic with his invitation, and he'd tried to decide when to tell her why they were making the trip. For too long he'd dealt with the old issues rioting in his mind. If shame and guilt were tangled in his business, then he needed to take care of it. He realized he needed to be honest with Alissa and to make amends. Though it was too late to apologize to his father, his mother would be grateful, and he sensed the Lord would be pleased with his decision.

"Are you upset with me?" He realized he'd jerked Alissa from her thoughts.

She looked at him, confusion filling her eyes. "I don't like surprises. I'd rather know what's going on than to spend the whole trip trying to guess why this is so important. I've been here before. I saw your packinghouse, the orchard, and your home already. It's not that I didn't enjoy myself last time, but I'm edgy."

He drew up his shoulders. "We're not going to San Luis Obispo."

She turned on him as if he were a kidnapper. "I thought you said we were going to your house."

"I did, and we are."

She shook her head and looked out the passenger window. "You're talking in circles, Ross. I don't want to play games."

"This is no game, Alissa. I wanted you to see the place before I explained, but maybe I'm doing it backward. I'm not good with women, I guess."

"Yes, you are when you're acting normal. Since yesterday you've been somebody else."

Maybe he had. "It's a long story, so let me get started. I also have a business in Paso Robles. I'm sure I told you, and that's where I live most of the time."

"What?"

He nodded. "My mom has a place there, too, although I've

been thinking about having her live with me now that she's had this accident."

"What kind of business? More avocados?"

"No, and that's been my problem." The memories came crashing back, two bullheaded Cahills, each trying to prove to the other he was right.

"Then what? Just tell me. Is it illegal? Like drugs?"

His heart ached for her fears. Leading her on had been a mistake. "It's grapes."

"Grapes?" She gazed at him, more confusion filling her eyes. "What's wrong with grapes?"

"They're for making wine."

She shook her head as if trying to clear away the cobwebs. "Right, but people eat them, too."

"Mine are wine grapes. They're different."

"Oh."

"Do you see my problem?"

She looked out the passenger window a moment. "Jesus made wine."

"First, I don't make wine—I just grow the grapes. And second, yes, Jesus turned water into wine, but many Christians believe drinking is a sin because it leads to trouble and addiction."

"It can. I know. I don't drink, but some people don't think it's wrong."

"My family does. I do, and my dad was staunch about it."

She shifted beneath the seat belt to face him. "So is this what's been troubling you? Did you and your father have a falling-out?"

"My dad loved me, but he was set against my buying into the wine-grape business. He advised me not to, and he had good reason. Drunks ruin lives."

Alissa gasped and covered her mouth, her eyes filled with understanding. "Your brother."

She startled him. "You know about my brother?"

She lowered her hand. "Your mom told me about him one day."

"Do you know that he—"

"Yes." She closed her eyes. "It was a tragedy."

"So you can see how my dad hated the business, and it did put a barrier between us. He tried to be the same dad, but he couldn't forget what I'd done." Ross released the steering wheel from his left hand and massaged the tension in his neck. "I dropped a wall between us with that decision, and when my dad died three years later, I wondered if I'd been to blame."

Alissa opened her eyes. Moisture clung to her lashes. "No, Ross. I'm sure that had nothing to do with it, but I can understand how it might make you feel guilty. It's just that you and your dad weren't looking at the business in the same way."

"Right. I was looking at the profit. He was looking at it as a moral issue—a faith issue, really."

Alissa remained silent but reached over and rested her hand on his arm.

"It's a lucrative business," he added, "but not when it's started bothering me so much. It's not worth the money or the pain. Lately I realize how often I don't tell people about the grapes. I always say I'm in avocados. I never know when I'm talking to Christians who might be offended. It's gotten worse the longer I've let that happen, and I know I can't go on like this."

"If you're ashamed, then you know you're doing wrong."

He nodded, facing the truth. "I've known this for a while now, but it's my business, and I couldn't see changing it. The equipment costs so much, and trying to change the product wouldn't be worth it. I really want to get rid of the business. I know many people enjoy wine and don't find it a sin. And the Bible says Jesus turned water into wine, as you mentioned, but I don't want to be that person."

"Why now? What's made the difference?"

"You."

She drew back, her eyes searching his. "Me? I never said anything about—"

"Because I didn't tell you, and I've told you everything about me, Alissa, except that. It made me realize I'm doing something I know is wrong. It's not just Roger's death or his addiction. It's my faith. The two just don't go together."

Alissa fell silent, and Ross speculated on what she was thinking. His admission could have turned her against him, or, he hoped, she comprehended his remorse.

"What will you do?" she said finally.

"I don't know what to do. I wish I hadn't made the decision, but I did, so it's too late to alter that. But I can do something. It's what I have to decide."

She nodded and became thoughtful again.

The scenery passed by, and once through San Miguel, he knew they were getting close. Before Paso Robles, Ross veered off on a side road leading up into the hills, where terraced grapevines flourished on both sides of the road. When he came to his sign, PROSPERO VINEYARDS, he took a right and wound his way through the tree-lined road to his house.

When they came through the trees into the circular driveway, Alissa gasped. "This is your home?"

"Welcome to Cahill Ranch."

She sat there as if stunned.

Ross walked to the passenger side and opened the door. "Alissa?"

She turned toward him. "It's gorgeous. All of this is your house?"

He nodded. "My office is a little distance from here."

She didn't move.

"Are you getting out?"

"I'm startled. This has been too much of a surprise for me."

He took her elbow and helped her out, standing beside her as she studied the rambling stucco home with a wide courtyard entrance, the fountain he loved sending water over its spout to the wide basin below. Wind chimes tinkled in the breeze, music to his ears. He loved this place and couldn't imagine ever finding a home as satisfying. "Let's go inside."

Alissa looked at him then gazed at the entrance and took a step forward as if questioning every step.

❧

"I've never seen anything more wonderful," Alissa said, turning full circle to survey the wide entrance with curved staircases on both sides heading to the upper rooms. Ahead she viewed a great room, its ceiling soaring upward, enhanced by a stone fireplace that rose to the rafters with an expanse of windows on both sides offering a view of the landscape and the foothills beyond.

"I love it here," Ross said, his voice filled with nostalgia.

Alissa stepped forward, questioning her wisdom to tell him what she'd thought when she visited San Luis Obispo. He'd talked about being open, and she decided to do the same. "When I visited your other house, I was surprised it wasn't more elegant. It is very lovely with the cathedral ceiling and skylights. The view is similar to this one, but less scenic. I'd imagined that if you owned an avocado ranch, you would be rich, and the house didn't quite fit the mold."

"I don't fit the mold either." He stepped closer to her and rested his hands on her shoulders.

"This house fits the mold, even if you don't." She grinned, hoping to bring a smile to his face.

"I'll give you the grand tour later, but come with me." He beckoned her to follow.

He led her through a doorway on the side of the great room into a formal dining room and then into the most tremendous kitchen she'd ever seen.

A woman stepped through a doorway across the room, her dark eyes crinkling with her smile. "I heard your voices."

"*Hola*, Carmelita."

"Hola, Mr. Cahill. You're right on time."

"This is Alissa Greening, the woman I told you about."

"*Mucho gusto.*"

"It's nice to meet you, too," Alissa said.

Ross rested his hand on Alissa's shoulder. "Carmelita is my housekeeper and cook."

"I have your lunch almost ready, but if you'd like to go out on the patio, I'll bring some appetizers."

Ross moved toward her and gave her a hug. "You're a gem. *Gracias.*" He grasped Alissa's hand and steered her toward a sliding door.

When they stepped outside, she drew in the scent of foliage and the sweet fragrance of grapes. Looking past the landscape, she saw the terraced hills beyond. "Your vineyard?" She pointed to the neat rows of vines clinging to supports.

"That's it." He motioned toward an umbrella table then pulled out her chair so she sat facing the distant hills. Shadowed by the umbrella, Alissa felt a soft breeze whisper through her hair, and she imagined what it might be like to live in this house...and with a housekeeper, of all things.

"I don't travel much since I've owned the inn, so this is a treat. Being served by someone in a private home is unbelievable." She looked from him to the landscape and back. "And you live like this every day."

He nodded. "God has been good to me, even with my mistakes."

"We all falter, Ross." She rested her hand on his. "This is so special for me, and I can't imagine your having to give this up."

His eyes filled with sadness. "I can't either."

"Could you sell the vineyard and keep the house?"

He shook his head. "The house is part of the land. They go together. Whatever I do, the two stay together."

Sadness washed over her, seeing his despondency. Though his decision to buy the vineyard had been one some people might call careless, Alissa understood why he'd purchased it. Besides the income, the area was gorgeous, its rugged landscape an amazing demonstration of God's creation, with the mountains and lush soil and the ocean only a few miles away. She couldn't be angry with him, and his dilemma broke her heart.

"Here you are," Carmelita said, approaching them.

Alissa turned as the woman neared them with a tray. She rested it on the table and set a tall glass of iced tea garnished with lemon and mint leaves in front of her with a bowl of guacamole and a basket of homemade corn chips. Another bowl of salsa filled out the treats.

"This is great," Alissa said to the woman. "Thank you."

Carmelita grinned and dug into her pocket. "I'm supposed to give you this." She handed Alissa an envelope then smiled at Ross and headed back inside.

Alissa eyed the envelope then turned it over in her hand. "What's this?"

Ross chuckled. "Open it."

She undid the flap and pulled out a recipe card. The words PRIZE-WINNING GUACAMOLE were written across the top. "I forgot to get this the last time. This is your recipe, isn't it?"

"It's the one I told you about." He gestured toward the bowl on the table. "Try it."

Alissa reached for a corn chip and dug it into the avocado mixture then took a bite. The taste tingled in her mouth, a delightful mix of the fruit with spices and citrus. She took another bite, loving the flavor of lime and cilantro, the zest of chilies and onion and refreshing bits of tomato. "It's delicious."

"I thought you'd like it, and now you can make it yourself."

"You know I will." She grasped another chip and dipped it into the guacamole.

Ross joined her, and they nibbled the appetizers, avoiding any more sad talk.

The unpleasant topic remained unspoken through dinner. Carmelita prepared chicken flautas with Mexican rice, a tempting mix of grilled chicken, peppers, and onions with cumin and other spices. The meal would have been perfect except for their earlier conversation weighing on her mind.

When they prepared to leave, Alissa admired the lovely home, the second floor with its massive bedrooms and spacious baths and a home office on the first floor, so lovely her own heart ached for Ross's decision.

Alissa felt sad when the topic came up again on the way home.

"I hope you understand why I didn't mention this business, Alissa. As we've become so close, I knew I had to be open with you, and I needed you to understand what's bothering me and how I allowed material things to influence my faith."

She wanted to say something to soothe his regret. "It's easy to do, Ross. I think we all make those horrible mistakes. While we were there, I had thoughts of my own. In a way, I did something similar to what you did. Fern was set against my selling the family property. Mom's house would have been a lovely bed-and-breakfast, and it was closer to the downtown area so it had that good feature, but I wanted to be classier. I knew I could make more money having an inn on the ocean's doorstep, and I set up all those rules for myself—home-baked cookies, afternoon snacks, flowers and fruit bowls in each room."

"But all those things make your place unique. You can't be upset for that."

Alissa pressed her hand against her chest, emotions billowing as she spoke to him with frankness. "The point is, I hurt my sister by making that decision." A sense of sorrow crept through her as she studied Ross. "The difference is, I have time to say I'm sorry and to make amends. You don't."

He nodded. "That hurts even more than selling the property." He lifted his hand and made small circular motions on his temple as if to chase away a headache.

Her temple pulsed, as well. "I can't imagine your going through with this, Ross. I really can't."

"I can't either, Alissa. I really can't."

ten

Ross stood in the doorway of his mother's room at the nursing home and watched her a moment. She'd made excellent improvements, beyond the physician's expectations, but she still needed care. He'd been spending time dealing with one dilemma after another. First, he needed to find someone to care for his mother or he needed to accept Alissa's offer to care for her. That seemed unfair to Alissa, and he feared his mother would feel abandoned.

Next, he struggled with his property in Paso Robles—his home, his vineyards, his life in that city—and finally, Alissa. His feelings had grown beyond friendship or attraction. He'd fallen in love. The idea seemed preposterous, but as he'd said so often, with God all things were possible. He'd felt the Lord guiding him very soon after he met Alissa. Her values and personality fit his so well, but their careers created a towering wall holding them back from finding a solution.

He could never ask Alissa to give up her inn. It meant so much to her, and he knew she would never ask him to give up his livelihood. God had the answer, but Ross didn't.

His mother glanced toward the door and smiled. "How long have you been standing there?"

"A couple of minutes. You were so engrossed."

She waved the little book toward him. "Crossword puzzles. Alissa brought me this the other day. It certainly helps to pass the time, when they're not torturing me."

"That's called therapy, Mom." He crossed the room and kissed her cheek. "I suppose this box of candy can't compete with that puzzle book."

"Try me." She extended her hand and accepted the chocolates. "No nuts. Good. I prefer the nougat and cream centers."

"That's why I bought them." He pulled a chair closer, slipped off his jacket, and sat beside her. "How was therapy today?"

"Good. I even tackled a few steps. It's a challenge."

He leaned back in the chair. "You know they're sending you home in a few more days. You should be home by Thanksgiving."

"I heard, and I can't wait." She tossed the puzzles onto her bedside table. "Everyone's nice here, but it's still too much like a hospital."

"I think I'll have you stay with me. I'll put a hospital bed in my downstairs office, and I'll hire someone to care for you during the day. I could ask Carmelita, but I think that's—"

His mother held up her hand. "Whoa! Slow down."

Her determined voice surprised him. "What?"

"Did you ask me what I want to do?"

He squirmed, feeling as he had when he was a troublesome teenager. "I want to do what's best for you, and I thought—"

"If my brain stopped working, you'd have the right to make decisions for me. I have that in my living will. But now you can discuss things with me."

He knew he was in for a battle. "What don't you like about my idea, Mom?"

"First, your telling me what I'm going to do."

"Okay." He stopped himself from rolling his eyes. "What else?"

"I don't want to go to your house. That's not home."

He released an exasperated sigh. "If you go to your home, you'll have to have twenty-four-hour care with strangers. I can afford that, Mom, but I thought you'd want to be with someone who cared about you."

"I do want that."

"You want me to move into your house?" He pictured her small condo a few miles from his place. Though staying with her would be inconvenient, he would make the arrangements. "Okay. I can do that."

"You're not the only one who cares about me."

Her comment struck him between the eyes. *Alissa.* "You mean—"

"Alissa offered me a room, and I feel very much at home there. She's a beautiful person, and I enjoy her company."

He stood and walked across the room and back, trying to figure out how to say what he had to say in a nonaggressive way. "Don't you think that's asking a lot of Alissa? She really doesn't know us that well. We're guests in her inn. She's kind, but—"

His mother shook her head. "Are you trying to pull the wool over my eyes?"

"The wool? What are you talking about?"

"You and Alissa are in love. She'll be my daughter-in-law soon enough, and this is a wonderful way for me to get to know her better."

His pulse kicked into high speed. "Who told you we're in love?"

"I have a bum hip, Ross. I'm not blind. Anyone can see—"

"We've never talked of love. Never."

"You don't have to. Look at your sleeve. It's written all over that and your face. The two of you were meant for each other. Don't tell me you haven't figured that out yet."

He sank back into the chair with the truth ringing in his ears. He'd fallen hard and fast, and he had no idea what to do about it.

"Cat got your tongue?" she asked.

"No. I'm just surprised."

She chuckled. "Surprised that your mother can still read your mind after all these years?" She wagged her finger at him. "You were never good at lying, Ross, and you were never good at hiding your mistakes. I knew when you took a dollar from some change on the table and bought candy. I knew when you told me someone vandalized your bicycle that you and Butchy had tried to do some foolish tricks with it by jumping off a hill. You could have killed yourself."

Ross looked to his right, expecting to see a jury tallying up his "guilty" points. "How did you know all that? And it wasn't Butchy. It was that kid whose father owned the bakery."

"So I got that wrong." She waved it away.

He laughed at the expression on her face.

"I knew you weren't in love with Audra. Not the way a man should be."

A chill rolled down his back. Why had she known and he hadn't?

"Ross, I've never told you this, because I thought if I interfered, you wouldn't listen anyway and would be more set for the marriage. I prayed you would figure it out on your own, and you did. That marriage would have been a disaster."

"You really think so?"

"I just told you I do. But this one—you and Alissa—it's made in heaven, if ever a marriage was."

"We're not married, Mom. We're not even engaged. We've never spoken of marriage for that matter."

"No, but you will, and that's why I want to stay with Alissa. I'll pay for my room and my care. You don't need me to leave money to you. You're a wealthy man."

He opened his mouth and closed it, knowing he'd lost the battle.

"Good. No argument." Her eyes twinkled, and then she patted the arm of her chair. "Now that we have that settled, let's talk about your other problem."

"What other problem?"

"Business, I think. I know you're worried about where you

two will live, but just remember the Lord guides your steps. A verse in Hebrews says, 'I will put my trust in him.' That will work out with time, but you have a business problem. Tell me about it."

Air escaped his lungs as he searched her face, wondering when she'd learned to be a mind reader, or was that an attribute God gave mothers?

❧

"Do you see the boxes?" Alissa called through the opening as she stood below the drop-down ladder while Ross rummaged through her attic. She didn't hear anything. "I can come up."

Ross looked over the edge, holding a carton of wreaths. "How do you do this each year?"

She shrugged. "Determination, and I have to for the guests. Anyway, Fern usually helps."

He handed down the cumbersome box then shifted away from the opening. She heard a rustle, and soon he reappeared with another carton. "And *why* do you do this?"

She chuckled at his taunting. "Christmas is coming, for one, and the other, Butterfly Trees is part of the Christmas-at-the-Inn event. It's an honor."

"For whom?"

This time she laughed. She raised her arms to reach for the carton then set it down, while he hurried off for another box. She had five, maybe six boxes filled with holiday decorations, not counting the huge outdoor wreath she kept in a storage area off her kitchen.

When he'd unloaded the boxes, Alissa left one upstairs with the decorations for that floor, and they carried down the others. With Thanksgiving in a few days, the inn was empty for a change, and she was grateful. "Your mom's released on Wednesday?"

"Right," he said, undoing the flaps of a carton and looking inside.

"That gives me two days to get these Christmas decorations up."

"And I can't help tomorrow. I have an appointment."

"Appointment? Down in Paso Robles or—"

"No, it's in this area. I won't be gone the whole day, I don't think."

A local appointment made her curious, but she sensed she shouldn't ask. His business wasn't her business. She let her questions fade and flagged him to follow. "Let's look at your mother's room, and tell me what you think."

He dropped the garland he'd untangled across the chair and joined her. "You really care what I think?"

She knew he was teasing. "This is in regard to your mother, so I hope so." She opened the door of the Painted Lady Room and stepped inside. "Look around and tell me if you think everything is out of the way for her to get around. I removed all the scatter rugs so she won't trip."

Ross grasped her hand and pulled her to him, his look so tender she felt weak. "You're an angel, Alissa."

"No, I'm not. I like your mother. Love her, really. She's sweet and spunky both. I love that in her, and I don't want her to get discouraged. She'll enjoy sitting out in the ·parlor and talking with guests. They'll think she's my mother. She won't be a problem at all."

"And I'll sleep at night knowing she's with someone who loves her."

"I'm glad. That's what I want for you. I know you have lots of things on your mind."

He nodded, his gaze searching hers until he lifted her chin with his finger and lowered his lips to hers.

Their lips fit perfectly, gentle and sweet like honey on a spoon. He drew her closer, his arms against her back, and she breathed in his woodsy citrus scent she'd learned to love. She'd learned to adore everything about Ross, even his pensive moments when he struggled with his thoughts.

He drew back, his lips so close she could feel the whisper of his breath. "I'm crazy about you."

She wanted to cry out that she felt the same, but her heart and mind wrestled with reason and emotion. She'd prayed, but no answer had come. "You mean so much to me, too. I'm glad your mother's here, because it means you'll be here."

"I could be with you always, Alissa, if you want it to be."

"If we want it to be, but I have no answers, Ross." She drew back, sorry the lovely moment had ended and they were back to reality. "We have careers we've both worked hard for, and I've prayed, but I'm not sensing an answer."

He grasped her hands and pressed them against his chest. "I've prayed, too. We can't find the answer alone, but I believe God has led us to this place in our lives. The other day my mom talked about us, and she said—"

"Your mother?"

A crooked grin stole to his lips. "You know mothers. They think they know everything." He shook his head. "And sometimes they do. Anyway, she reminded me of a Bible verse that's so simple but one we need to listen to. 'I will put my trust in Him.'"

The verse seemed too easy. "I trust the Lord. I really do, but—"

He pressed his finger against her lips. "There's your problem. Trust means no buts. I'm talking seriously for once. We need to trust without the buts."

She rested her head against his chest, feeling safe in his arms, and knew she should feel safe in God's arms, as well.

They stood in the room with the sunlight streaming through the window, and Alissa could see the rugged shoreline outside washed in the waves that pounded against it. The rocks were strong and steadfast as was the Lord. Today she felt as safe as the seals who lolled there in the sun.

"The room looks great," Ross whispered in her ear. "Everything is perfect. The hallway is wide enough, and Mom will enjoy sitting here in the wingback chair."

His words brought her back, but the word *trust* remained in her heart. "I found a footstool in another room for her. She may want to prop up her feet." She motioned to the blue upholstered ottoman she'd located that nearly matched the blue in the chair.

"You think of everything."

"Speaking of everything, I have work to do." She eased back and headed for the door.

"*We* have work. It'll take you weeks to do that decorating alone."

Happiness wrapped around her, and she felt like skipping down the hallway like a girl.

The tasks began as Alissa hung wreaths in every window and arranged a single candle on each windowsill while Ross set a ladder against the inn to hang the huge wreath that sparkled with miniature lights on the gable of the porch. He festooned the porch railing with garland and ribbons while she moved from room to room with holiday pillows and special wreaths designed for each door featuring a butterfly for which the room had been named.

Enjoying the partnership, she made hot chocolate and carried a mug outside for Ross. Even without snow and the bitter chill of winter found in most states, Alissa felt the spirit of Christmas. Ross tackled his last task, hanging the cluster of bells on the door so it jingled when people came inside.

He lowered the hammer. "I've never done this before."

She felt her nose wrinkle. "You've never hung bells?"

He chuckled. "I've never hung anything. Bachelors don't decorate for holidays."

"What about when—" That would have been a mistake, and she stopped herself.

"Audra?"

She nodded.

"Audra decorated her place and carried on because I didn't. One time she brought me a real pine tree in a pot with a string of lights."

Alissa didn't want to know about the sweet things Audra did. "That was nice."

"She was embarrassed because I was hosting a party for her friends. Audra had Carmelita decorate the dining room table to her specifications. I don't know why I didn't care."

Because you didn't love her. Alissa had watched him lug the decorations out of the attic to the first floor, hang wreaths, wrap garland around the long porch, and hang the bells. He did that for her without her even asking. Her heart stretched with awareness, and she wrapped her arms around his neck. "Thank you for doing this."

"It was fun." He opened the door, listening to the jingling bells. "Now show me what you did."

"I'm not quite finished, but I will be."

"We will be." He curved his arm around her waist, and they headed inside.

&

"Are you okay, Mom?" Ross slipped the ottoman closer to the chair then pressed his lips to her cheek. "It's good to see you home."

Home. The inn had almost become home to him. Here he found the feeling of comfort and completeness he'd missed for so many years. And here he found Alissa. She'd become his light at the end of a lonely tunnel, and she'd helped him focus on what was important.

"It's good to be here," his mother said, sending him a tender grin. "The only frustration I have is I'd like to help with the cooking for Thanksgiving tomorrow."

"I'm sure you can help with something. We'll see what

Alissa needs. You can stand now, and you can definitely sit."

She chuckled. "I'm good at sitting. . .and taking naps."

"Naps help to make you well." He squeezed her shoulder. "But walking is the important thing. Your therapist will be here soon."

"I can walk now, and I'm getting stronger," she said. She gazed toward the window. "I love this view. It's so beautiful, and I'm grateful I had a chance to see the monarch butterflies before I decided to take my last trip."

"Your last trip?" It took him a moment to understand, and he laughed. "You mean your trip over the rock."

She nodded. "That's one trip I don't want to repeat." She pointed through the window. "But this is one I could enjoy often."

"I know." His chest tightened. "I love you, Mom," he said, giving her a wave. "Alissa has me lined up for tree decorating."

"It's about time. I never saw anyone who avoided putting up decorations as you do." She grinned. "I guess Alissa has found the secret of motivation."

He knew she had something on her mind.

"Love does wonderful things."

He gave her a scowl and shook his finger. "We've never talked about that."

"It's about time you did."

He shook his head and stepped into the corridor, very aware that his mother, as always, was absolutely correct.

When he entered the parlor, he saw the bare evergreen standing beside the stair railing, and he knew he was supposed to string the lights. He could smell something wonderful drifting in from the kitchen, and he pushed open the door—no need for guest protocol anymore—and gazed at Alissa. "What are you doing?"

"Making cookies. I need refreshments for the Christmas-at-the-Inn event, and I thought I'd get started."

"You said you were making pies."

"That's next." She scratched her chin with her knuckle and left a white splotch of flour. "How's your mom?"

"Spunky as ever. Her therapist will be here soon, and I hope she isn't too achy afterward." He walked closer and brushed the white dust from her face.

"Do you think she'd like to help out here?"

"She'd love it. Ask her. She mentioned feeling disappointed she couldn't help."

"Good," Alissa said. "I'll see how she feels after therapy."

Her expression changed, and Ross felt uneasy with her look.

"Where did you go yesterday? You usually talk about your business, and you didn't this time."

He knew it. "I visited a ranch in Watsonville."

"Watsonville? That's the 'Strawberry Capital of the World.' Do they have avocados there, too?"

"Watsonville has all kinds of produce. I was visiting a ranch to see how they handle the business. I always learn new things to improve my companies." He'd told her the truth but left out some things. He didn't want to give her hopes he couldn't fulfill.

"Good idea since you're this far, I suppose." She still looked suspicious, but she didn't question him further and slipped a tray of cookies into the oven.

"I'll sit with Mom and wait for the therapist, or if you tell me where the Christmas tree lights are, I'll string them."

"They're in a box near the registration desk. Thanks. I'll come out and help when I get this last batch finished."

He slipped through the door and spotted the box she'd mentioned. As he untangled the long strands of lights, Ross reviewed what he'd heard and seen yesterday in Watsonville. Although he knew nothing about strawberries, he could learn, and buying the farm would bring him closer to Pacific

Grove. He'd still have his home in San Luis Obispo when he needed to be down there.

Selling Prospero Vineyards and the ranch cut deep. He could give up the vineyard; he loved his home there, though, and he suspected he'd never find another as special. Still, he wanted to make a change, and this seemed a possibility.

Before he unknotted the third string, Ross heard the doorbell ring. He dropped the strand and opened the door, hearing the bells jangle. "You're the therapist?"

The young woman nodded and introduced herself.

"Glad you found us," he said, pushing the door open. "Mom's right down this corridor."

"Thanks," she said.

He led the way then tapped on the door and heard his mother's voice. Ross pushed it open. "The therapist is here."

The woman walked inside and set her bag on a table near the door. "Hi, Mrs. Cahill. I'm Kim Roland. Ready for a workout?"

His mother quipped a comment, and he chuckled as he turned away. He would rather untangle Christmas tree lights than watch his mom be in pain. Grasping a string of lights, he went back to work. He looped the white lights around his hand and began the task of draping them over the tree branches. The tree looked real, but Alissa had purchased a quality artificial tree, she'd explained, knowing it would last through the lengthy time it would stand in the parlor.

When he neared the bottom, Alissa came in from the kitchen. "It looks great." She motioned toward his mother's bedroom. "How's Maggie doing?"

"I'm not sure, but I haven't heard any screams yet."

She waved his words away with the shake of her head. "I'll check."

She bounced across the room then turned to face him. "Coward." She made a cute face and flitted away.

He looked at the Christmas tree and grinned.

eleven

Alissa stood in the doorway, watching Maggie with the therapist a few moments before she interrupted. "How's it going?"

"Good," the therapist said, introducing herself. "She's really strong for her age, and—"

"What do you mean, for my age?"

Maggie had a twinkle in her eye, and Alissa chuckled at the surprised look on the therapist's face; then the young woman caught on and laughed with them.

"I see you're walking well," Alissa said. "Could you help me with the pies later?"

"Pies? I'd love to."

"Maggie's doing amazingly well, and she can do a lot of things, but she needs to take a few precautions." The therapist gave Maggie a stern look. "No crossed legs and no reaching past your knees or between your legs. When standing, don't lean forward, and avoid sitting on low, soft chairs. Otherwise, if you're not in pain, then go for it."

"I'll be jumping rope in a week or two," Maggie said, her optimism heightening.

"I think it'll be a number of months before you'll be doing that," Kim said, "but you're on your way if you keep doing your exercises." Kim looked toward Alissa. "The main activity is walking. In another week or so, she needs to get outside with the walker. Get used to walking there."

"We'll help with that," Alissa said, smiling and stepping away. She returned to the living room, where Ross had finished the lights and begun stringing garland that looked like cranberries. "Let me help." She grasped the loop of beads, and they passed it back and forth as they wound their way to the bottom.

"Now that's the way to do it," Ross said. "It's easier with two." He slipped beside her and tilted her chin upward. "Many things are. Remember the animals filled the ark two by two."

"I remember reading about that," she said, eyeing the hallway for the therapist. She gave him a teasing frown, and he leaned down and gave her a quick kiss on the end of her nose.

"Let's get serious," she said.

"I was. I'm being very serious."

Though he was being playful, Alissa sensed his comment meant more than decorating the tree. She'd been dealing with her emotions for weeks now, knowing she'd fallen in love; she loved the inn, though, and he loved and needed his work. These were their livelihoods.

With God all things are possible. The words nettled her like a bee sting. She reeled back from the unexpected revelation. Maybe the good Lord had to smack people in the head once in a while just to keep them on their toes. God had an answer. She would have to wait patiently for it.

Forcing her mind away from her thoughts, Alissa delved into decorating the Christmas tree. She loved the Victorian-style ornaments she'd purchased over the years—ones that looked like home-baked cookies, metal designs, crocheted angels, and amazing paper baubles. She'd found cloth balls that looked like patchwork and needlepoint squares at the craft show. She thought now they were finished, but when she looked up, Ross had found some pinecones adorned with paint and glitter.

He held one up, eyeing it. "I could have made this."

"Then I'll get you a booth at the craft show next year."

They laughed, and just as he'd stepped toward her with

that mesmerizing look in his eyes, the therapist strode into the room.

"I'll be leaving. I'd like you to encourage Maggie to do her foot pumps and ankle rotations and especially the knee bends." She described how they were to be done safely. "And walking. She can walk around her room and up and down the hallways with her walker. Another month or more on that, and then we'll see how a cane works." Her eyes widened as she turned and glanced over her shoulder. "For an older woman, she's doing extremely well."

"Mother's determined," Ross said. "She'll get well or else."

"Don't let her overdo it—and don't tell her she's doing well for her age. She doesn't like that."

Alissa and Ross chuckled at the same time.

The therapist left, and when Alissa went to check on Maggie, she found her lying on the bed with a quilt over her knees. "I'm going to take a little nap. Can we do the pies later?"

"Absolutely. You're not holding me up at all. Ross and I are decorating the tree." .

Maggie released a soft chuckle. "If you only knew him a year ago, Alissa, you'd know he is a different man." She gave Alissa a tender look. "Thank you."

Alissa watched Maggie close her eyes, letting what she'd said soak in. *A different man.* She recalled when he first arrived at the inn, the night he checked in late, and he was very different then. He'd arrived like a chrysalis, and he'd opened up to become a magnificent butterfly—an emperor butterfly—just like the name of his room.

Gathering her thoughts, she returned to the parlor. Ross had disappeared, and she figured he was upstairs. She headed for the kitchen, and when she opened the door, she found him inside preparing hot chocolate.

"I hope you don't mind. I hung those pinecones, so we're finished, and this tasted so good earlier. I thought we could just sit for a while and enjoy the tree lights."

"I don't mind at all, and I'll steal a few of those Christmas-at-the-Inn cookies."

"Great." He motioned to the doorway. "I want to get something in my room. I'll be down in a minute to finish."

Alissa placed the cookies on a plate then set it and the mugs on a tray, but before she could carry them into the parlor, Ross appeared and took the tray from her. She held open the swinging door and followed past the tree while Ross set the tray on the low table.

Alissa settled on the love seat, admiring the old-fashioned Christmas tree with a hand-crafted angel on top. The metal ornaments glittered with tiny white lights. They'd attached a few clip-on candle ornaments with lights inserted so the Christmas tree had the look of a Victorian tree with real candles burning.

"Since it's almost Christmas, I thought—"

Alissa chuckled. "You sound like a little kid. Christmas is a month away."

"You'd hardly know it with all these decorations, so let's pretend it's Christmas."

She shrugged, not sure why it made any difference. "Okay. It's Christmas."

"Good," he said, pulling a bag from beside a chair. "Merry Christmas." He handed her the bag and settled back.

"What's this?"

"Open it, and you'll know."

She studied the unmarked sack, trying to image what it could be. Laughing at herself for dallying, she unwound the top and looked inside. "It's from the bazaar, isn't it?"

He grinned. "You liked it, and so did I."

She drew out the metal rod holding the lovely copper and black monarch butterfly. "It's beautiful, Ross. Thank you." She leaned over, kissing his cheek.

"That made it all worthwhile—the smile on your face and the kiss."

She rose and studied the Christmas tree. "I think I could stick it in the branches for now, and it'll look like an ornament."

"Sounds like an idea." He stood and helped her find the perfect spot then manipulated the stick through the branches while trying not to knock off any ornaments. When he finished, they stood back and admired the lovely decoration.

Alissa returned to her seat and grasped her hot chocolate. "Let's make a toast to a job well done," she said, lifting her mug.

"I'd rather toast to us."

Ross lifted his drink, and they clicked their mugs together; instead of bringing Alissa joy, though, the toast reminded her of their difficulty.

"Cheer up," Ross said, slipping his arm around her shoulder. "Answers will come. I know they will."

"I wish God would give us a little hint of how it can work out. You're not in a position to leave your businesses. They're successful because you run them with your wisdom and love. It's the same here. This place is my dream, and I—I don't know."

"You don't know about me?"

His expression looked strained, and her chest hurt from holding back her emotion. "It's not that. I think we should be friends. Good friends, and leave it at that. I don't want to be hurt."

"Neither do I, but friends? You mean I can't hold you in my arms. I can't kiss your sweet lips. Is that what you mean?"

She didn't know how to respond. Desperation swept over her, and she saw the same in Ross's eyes.

He set his mug on the table and leaned closer to her. "Do you care about me, Alissa? I mean, really care? Forget we've only known each other for a few weeks. It doesn't take a lifetime to find someone when God is the guide."

She faced him, trying to control the tears pushing against her eyes. "Do you have to ask?" She slid her mug onto the coffee table. "You know you've been the focus of my days. I feel empty when you're not here, and the only thing that helps is that I know you'll be back because I'm holding your mother captive."

Ross grasped her hand. "You didn't agree to keep my mother here because of that, did you?"

She flexed her palm upward at his joke. "Scout's honor. I've grown to love your mom, and I—I care about you. It's good for all of us. And your visiting is the bonus."

"What if we could be together every day? What if—"

She pressed her finger against his lips, unable to bear his pleading. "Don't." She closed her eyes, wrestling with the myriad of questions and thoughts bound inside. "What we have right now is wonderful. We're dearest friends. We enjoy each other's company. We laugh, we tease, and we have good talks. We share a faith. What more do we need?" Alissa knew what she needed, but all she had was an elusive dream that had no future.

"We need each other, Alissa. I didn't realize until meeting you that I want a real home and family. I want you to be part of that."

She sat a moment, hoping to find some way to sway him—to sway herself. "So do I," she whispered.

He shifted closer and drew her into his arms. "Then let's work this out. We can find a way. The answers are there if we want this bad enough."

She nodded, hoping he was right. She'd lived without love for so long. Alissa knew she could continue the same way, but now that she'd tasted the gift, could she let it go? "We need time to let things work."

"Until then I want us to remember that 'all things work together for good to them that love God.' Don't forget that."

"I won't."

"Tomorrow is Thanksgiving, and let's use that day to thank Him for our finding each other."

She managed a smile, and he leaned closer and pressed his lips to hers. She thawed in his arms, her cold fears fading and her prayers rising, and when Ross drew back, Alissa caught her breath. "If I don't get busy on the preparations, we'll be thankful tomorrow for a toasted cheese sandwich." She slipped from his grasp with a laugh. "You wouldn't want that, would you?"

He opened his arms. "If we could stay here forever, I wouldn't care."

"Phooey!" She skittered away, hoping the playful mood stayed with her. The dark feelings she'd had reminded her that life these past weeks had been unbelievable.

❧

Alissa put the last of the turkey in the freezer, though she'd left some in the refrigerator for sandwiches and a casserole. She put on the coffee and pushed open the swinging door. "Who's ready for dessert?"

She heard a playful groan coming from Ross. "I suppose I can force myself to have a piece."

She strode into the parlor. "How about you, Fern? Maggie?"

"I'll have a piece," Fern said.

Maggie nodded. "Just a sliver. The meal was delicious, but I want to see how my pies turned out."

"They look delicious. I'll whip the cream."

"Let me help," Ross said, jumping from the love seat and heading her way.

"He just wants to lick the beaters," Maggie called.

Fern laughed, and Alissa did, too, delighted Maggie had felt well enough to make the pies yesterday and had been so spirited today. She couldn't recall a time when her life had seemed so full.

Ross slipped in behind her and pushed the swinging door closed. He drew her into his arms and pressed his lips against her forehead. "This is a day to be thankful for. Mom's in fine spirits and is looking so good. Fern has been great, and we've come to somewhat of an agreement"—his smile inched to a scowl—"haven't we?"

"We have. I'm just scared. I don't want to get my heart broken."

"Neither do I, so I'm trusting in you, me, and the Lord."

She relaxed in his arms.

He shifted one arm and pulled up the edge of her lip. "There, that looks better. I see a smile."

She burst into laughter and sprang away. "No foolishness. We're here for the pies."

She grasped the cream then opened the freezer and pulled out the bowl and beaters. "You're in charge of the whipped cream while I cut the pie. Do you know how to hook in the beaters?"

As she lifted one, he pulled it from her fingers. "I had freshman home economics in high school. I'm a whiz."

She kept an eye on him while she pulled out the plates and cut the pie. When it was time for the sugar, she sprinkled a tablespoonful into the cream and let him finish the job.

"Done," he said, turning off the motor. "Look at this. Stiff peaks."

"Great job." She laughed as he pulled out the beaters, took a big lick off one, then pulled out the other and handed it to her.

She joined him as they gobbled up the delicious whipped topping. When she looked at him, she chuckled. He had white splotches above his lip and on his cheeks.

"You don't look any better, my dear." He turned her to face the toaster and lifted it for her to use as a mirror.

He was right. She grabbed a napkin and wiped her face then gave him a spoon to add the topping while she poured the coffee. Eventually they carried the drinks and dessert into the parlor while Maggie sat on a kitchen chair, her walker by her side, waiting patiently.

"I thought you'd decided to eat in there," Maggie said when they arrived.

"We had a whipped-cream battle," Ross said, handing her a piece.

Alissa handed Fern her piece and set the coffee mugs by each spot then dug into the pumpkin pie. She took a bite then another, feeling her eyes widen. "Maggie, this pie is outstanding. What did you do?"

"It's the orange zest. It really makes a difference."

"I guess."

"I thought pies were supposed to taste like this," Ross said, giving his mother a wink.

When they had finished, Alissa gathered the dishes while Ross helped his mother into the bedroom. Fern followed Alissa, and they piled the dishes into the dishwasher and cleaned up the kitchen.

"If you don't need me," Fern said, "I think I'll say good night to everyone."

"You've done enough. Thanks for helping clean up."

"This was great." Fern opened her arms, and Alissa gave her a big hug.

"It was nice, and you're always welcome."

"I feel welcome," Fern said, giving her an extra squeeze. "Love you."

"I love you, too," Alissa responded before Fern went into the parlor to say good night to Ross and Maggie. When she finished, Ross left the room while Alissa pulled the shades and helped Maggie get ready for bed, wrestling off the surgical compression stockings and helping her with her nightgown. After Maggie was tucked in, Alissa left her to sleep.

The day had been wonderful, and she hoped the evening

would go as well. They'd avoided talking about anything that would put a damper on the day. Their dinner blessing had been one of thanksgiving, and each had added a personal prayer of thanks. Fern's thanks had warmed Alissa's heart, and Maggie had thanked God for bringing Alissa into her life. She couldn't have asked for a better Thanksgiving.

Ross had spread out on the love seat, taking up the seat, so Alissa sank into a chair, studying his handsome face made more handsome by his loving spirit. He'd become a blessing in her life. They sat in silence for a while until Ross straightened and beckoned her to sit beside him.

"I didn't tell you earlier, but I'm leaving in the morning to go to the ranch. I have some things I need to handle, and I think you'll do better without me here during the Christmas-at-the-Inn event."

"You'll be gone that long?"

"It's not that long. I'll be back a couple of days after the event is over. Mom's doing well, and she doesn't need me, and you won't have to explain me to all the visitors."

"What do you mean, explain you? I'd love you to be here."

He shook his head. "Fern always helps you, and since I have things to attend to, it makes sense for me to go now."

"Is something wrong at the ranch?"

"No, everything's great. I talked with Hersh down in San Luis Obispo. Things are going smoothly, and Diaz says everything's fine, but I have paperwork and things to handle. I'll be back."

"I know. I have your mother hostage."

He laughed, and she managed to chuckle, too, but for some strange reason, she felt concerned about his leaving. Their talk the day before had been serious enough to affect them both. Each had hopes, but each had fears. At least she did, and if Ross were honest, he'd have to admit they had big decisions to make.

❧

"Thanks, Fern. I appreciate your coming back this morning to help clean up."

Her sister wiped another punch bowl cup and placed it in the box. "You're welcome. I knew you were tired last night after all your visitors from the Christmas-at-the-Inn event, and that's why I suggested we do it today."

"The two days went well, I thought."

Fern clasped another cup. "Very well. That cranberry apple punch was excellent. I think the lime slices added an extra zing."

"I thought so, too."

"And you really had a nice group," Fern said, placing the punch cup in the storage box.

"Ticket sales were good, as usual." She raised her shoulders in a sigh. "Looks like we're finished. I'll just run a dust cloth over the parlor. I saw some cookie crumbs."

"I'll do that. You take a break."

Alissa eyed her sister. "Why? You've helped enough. Everything's in good shape."

"Then why do you look so tense?"

Alissa raised her shoulders. "I'm not really tense. I'm—"

Fern shook her head. "Okay. Then you're uptight, agitated, stressed. You pick the right word."

Alissa felt helpless. "I suppose I am." She rested her elbow on the kitchen island and her cheek against her fist. "I have too much on my mind."

"Ross and what else?"

She heard a hint of satire in Fern's voice. "Ross and. . .Ross."

Fern snorted. "So what does that mean?"

"I don't know. I'm wondering why Ross left so abruptly and for so many days. He's been here faithfully since his mother's accident, and he left following a difficult discussion we had."

Her sister moved closer and stood beside her. "He proposed, and you refused?"

She could hardly speak. "Not exactly, but he talked about our future, and I don't see a future for us. It's too difficult. My work is here, and his is there."

"It's not on the moon, Alissa. It's a couple of hours away."

"I know, but—"

"I thought for sure you two were in love. Are you telling me it's one-sided?"

"No. It's not that."

Fern straightened and walked across the room then turned. "You're not making sense."

Alissa nodded. "I'm not making sense to myself." She raised her elbows from the counter.

Fern moved closer and rested her hands on Alissa's shoulders. "Love means giving and taking. It means compromise. I can't believe that if you truly love each other, you can't find a way to work through these problems."

Alissa pulled away, irritated at her sister's remark. "It may sound easy to you because this isn't your business. You didn't give up anything for this bed-and-breakfast, and I—"

"Hold on." Fern's eyes narrowed. "I didn't give up anything? I beg to differ. Our mother gave you our family home so you could have this place. You sold it. You took our family memories—the only thing we had left of Mom and Dad— and sold them to strangers because you wanted a classier place. You asked me to help you here when you needed someone, the pauper sister who'd lost money because of a scam artist she fell for. Even before you knew he was a crook, you begrudged my relationship with him, and you never let me forget it with your I-told-you-so attitude. Now you're telling me I never gave up anything."

Tears filled Alissa's eyes. "I never knew you felt that way about the house, Fern. I thought you resented Mom's giving the place to me and not to you."

"Never. I was proud you had a dream. I looked forward to

being a part of it with you, but you never let me. Only after I messed up did you ask me to work part-time, and you know what happened then. I never did anything to your liking." She held up her hand to keep Alissa from speaking. "But we've talked that through. It's forgiven, and I hope soon forgotten. I love this place. I'm proud of what you've done. When you need me, I'm here. I'd be happy to help fill in so you could spend more time with Ross." She lowered her hand and moved closer, her voice softening. "Alissa, I want you to be happy. At least one of us should be."

Alissa couldn't answer. She buried her face in her hands and wept.

Fern backed away and kept her distance for a while then drew nearer and wrapped her arm around Alissa's shoulders. "I love you, and I'm sorry I made you cry."

Her words of love brought Alissa another sob, and she buried her face against Fern's shoulder. When she'd contained her tears, she raised her head. "I love you, too, with all my heart."

"Aren't we silly?" Fern said, shaking her head.

The look on her face made Alissa chuckle, and in a moment, they were back in each other's arms but this time laughing.

When they had parted, Fern put her hands on her hips. "You've worked hard. The place looks wonderful, every room decorated. You still have cookies for the holidays. Ross should be here tomorrow. Maggie is doing well, and I'm here. Take a break. Go for a ride and think good things. And let me reassure you, Ross is a wonderful man. If he had to go away for a few days, he had good reason, and he'll be back, loving you as much as he did when he left. So go."

"Go where?"

Fern shrugged. "What place do you love around here? Take a walk on the pier. Go to the lighthouse. Visit Lovers' Point."

She chuckled. "Maybe not there. Wait until Ross is back."

"Asilomar. I'll take a walk on the beach. I could use some fresh air, and I love it there."

"Good, and cheer up while you're at it."

"I'll put on some running shoes. I haven't had any good exercise in a while."

"You'd better get it now because soon you'll have the Christmas visitors, and then you'll be busy."

"Thanks, Fern, and I really mean that."

"I know you do. Now get out of here. I'll take care of Maggie when she wakes from her nap. She's doing so well that she astounds me."

Alissa grinned. "Me, too, but not as much as this talk. You and I needed to have these talks years ago. I can't believe how people waste time harboring worries and grudges."

"Listen to yourself, Alissa. You're talking about wasting time. You have a man who's let you know he cares about you, and you're worried about Butterfly Trees Inn. This place will survive longer than you're here on earth."

Alissa stood a moment, her sister's words wending their way into her brain. *Wasting time.* That's what she'd been doing for too long. She loved her inn, but she cherished Ross. Which was more important? She didn't have to answer. The truth was in her heart.

As she approached the beach, Alissa's thoughts drifted from her conversation with Fern to a conversation she'd had with Ross. He'd said trust had no buts, and yet she'd continued to allow that word to permeate her thoughts and decisions.

The beach spread out before her as she slipped from the car and walked down to the sand. *Lord, clear my mind today just as the fresh air clears my lungs. Help me breathe in the truth.* As the words left her, something fluttered past. A dried leaf? A monarch butterfly? Life sometimes fluttered past, and if she didn't keep her eyes open, she'd miss something wonderful.

Her feet sank into the sand as she made her way toward the beach, and her eyes were dazzled by the sun glinting off the waves. She thought again of the monarch butterflies. Butterflies' lives were so short, but the Lord had given monarchs seven or eight months longer to live, long enough for them to make the journey back to their ancestors' winter home. Alissa had faith that God provided for the birds and the butterflies, as the Bible said, and He would provide for her, as well. Her heart leaped with the realization.

Why had she feared? Why had she put buts on every option? All she needed was faith and to wait patiently on the Lord's will.

⁂

Ross grinned as he headed down Highway 1. He'd been able to wrap up his business and even added a few things to his list, and he was still arriving in Pacific Grove a day early. He couldn't wait to see Alissa's surprised face.

Her face. He'd prayed and prayed the last few days that Alissa would see things as he did. He'd taken a leap of faith and made changes in his life, and it was almost too late to turn back. If Alissa let him down, he'd be hurt beyond belief. Still he'd resolved more than one issue since he'd left on Monday.

The radio played a love song, and Ross's pulse did a jog. He'd turned into a real romantic since he met Alissa. She'd grabbed his heart within a few days and hadn't let go. He whistled along with the tune, grinning to himself as he hit the town of Marina. Seaside was the next city then Monterey and Pacific Grove.

He tried to imagine what Alissa had been doing all morning. For the past two days, he knew, she'd been busy with the Christmas-at-the-Inn event. He'd avoided calling her, not wanting to lie if she asked him about his activities. Keeping secrets from her was difficult. He'd learned quickly she was a woman who wanted details.

The music cut off as a newscaster's voice interrupted the program. "Pacific Grove police are warning residents and guests to be alert for a possible mountain lion believed active in the beach tract and Asilomar area."

Beach tract and Asilomar. His brows tugged together with concern. He couldn't imagine Alissa being on the beach today following the inn event when she'd have cleaning up to do; however, an active mountain lion could wander around the beachfront homes, and he suspected she hadn't bothered to turn on the TV or radio.

The newscaster continued. "If you come upon a mountain lion, do not run. Face the animal and look into his eyes. Move slowly and make yourself appear as large as you can by standing on your tiptoes or spreading a jacket wider. Mountain lions will not attack if they believe they are in danger. These animals usually attack the head or neck, so avoid crouching, bending over, or sitting in lion country, especially if you are alone. These animals have been considered protected mammals in California since 1990, so their population has grown in the last eighteen years."

Though he'd hoped to surprise Alissa with his early return, Ross tossed the idea aside and pulled out his cell phone. He punched Alissa's speed dial number, his ear pressed to the receiver.

"Butterfly Trees Inn."

A charge of disappointment struck him. "Fern, this is Ross. Could I speak to Alissa?"

"Sorry, Ross. She's not here. She didn't take her cell phone either, because I see it on the registration desk."

"Is she shopping? I thought she'd be there today."

"We cleaned up the place, and your mom is napping, so she decided to get some exercise on the beach."

His heart flew to his throat. "The beach? Which one?"

"Is something wrong?"

"Which one?"

"She mentioned Asilomar."

"No."

"What's wrong?"

"A mountain lion's been spotted in that area."

"What should I do, Ross?"

"I'm on my way. You stay put. I'll head over there."

"I'll be praying," Fern said, her voice tense.

"Thanks. So will I."

Ross flipped the cell closed and tossed it on the passenger seat. "Lord, please keep her safe. There's a lot of beach, and I might be silly here, but I can't take chances. I love this woman. You know that because You can see into my heart. Thank You, Jesus, for Your protection."

He gripped the steering wheel and pressed his foot firmer against the accelerator. If he got a ticket, so be it. Then he'd have a police escort. . .at least he hoped.

When he hit the beach tract, he watched the road but glanced along the shoreline, his heart thundering. Maybe he was being foolish. Of all the people in the world, why would Alissa be the one to be on the beach at the very moment a mountain lion had also decided to wander along the shoreline?

The road curved, and he spotted the lighthouse and slowed. Traffic had thinned, so he took his time, even pulling off the road to scan the horizon. Fern had mentioned Asilomar, so he stepped on the gas and made his way to the Asilomar area. He parked on Sunset Drive, as close as he could get to the water, then spotted Alissa's sedan and knew he was in the right place.

Ross made his way toward the beach, his eyes shifting from right to left in search of a possible mountain lion. When he reached the crest of a grassy area, he spotted a lone figure running along the mile stretch of sand. *Alissa!* He recognized her shape and her buttery blond hair glowing in the early afternoon sun. She paused and stretched her arms upward, jogging in place.

He opened his mouth to call but thought better of it and stood at the higher point to scan the area. Below him on a lower crest, he saw a movement, or had it been sand swirling in the breeze? *No.* He narrowed his eyes. Something sand-colored moved forward. *The mountain lion!* Ross watched as the lion crouched in the mix of sand and grass, facing Alissa.

With his heart racing, Ross tried to remember what the newscaster had said. Although he knew the rules for encountering a dangerous animal, his senses had frozen and his mind reeled with fear. Recollection hit him. Convince the lion Alissa wasn't prey, but how could he do that? As his gaze darted toward Alissa, he noticed her sink Indian-style into the sand. *No!* His stomach churned. She'd chosen the worst position she could be in. As he snapped his head toward the lion, it crouched lower to the ground and began inching forward.

Alissa, please stand. Lord, give her an instinct to stand. She remained seated, still, her head bent forward as if in thought or prayer. *Stand up, Alissa.*

God, help me. As the prayer left him, the answer came. His only course of action was to draw the lion's attention to him. He could reach his car faster than Alissa. He closed his eyes and began to slip off his jacket; then in the loudest voice he could summon, he screamed toward the lion.

twelve

A man's cry jarred the silence. Alissa pivoted her head and saw a man slipping off his jacket. *Ross.* What was he doing? He raised it over his head, whirling it in the air. She followed the direction of his eyes, and her knees weakened. A mountain lion was heading for Ross!

Her pulse escalated, leaving her breathless. Had it been heading for her? She could only guess. She rose slowly and headed upward toward the grassy knoll but kept her distance. Ross stood between her and the animal.

Ross yelled again as he moved forward, flapping his jacket. The lion settled into a crouch.

Alissa whispered a prayer. "Lord, please. No." Her breath left her as she made her way up the hill, trying to be unobtrusive yet ready to draw the lion to her rather than seeing Ross lose his life to save hers.

Ross bellowed again, and the cat raised it's head, its back twisting as it turned and sped away from them across the grass.

"Ross." Her voice penetrated the sound of the surf, and he turned, bounding down the sand dune to meet her. She flew into his arms and buried her face in his chest. Her fear released in hot tears.

Ross's body trembled beside her, their emotion at high pitch. "Thank You, Lord," he said, rocking her against him. "I couldn't believe what I saw. I can't believe I could have lost you."

"How did you know I was here?"

He eased back to look at her. "I heard a police report bulletin on the radio about a mountain lion spotted in this area, and I began to worry it would wander too close to the inn, so

I called. Fern told me you were here."

"You weren't supposed to come until tomorrow."

He released a pent-up breath. "I know. God works in amazing ways. I planned to surprise you. My business was finished, and I couldn't wait to see you."

"You did surprise me," she said, trying to make light of the horrible experience. "I've never seen a mountain lion. I know they can come this far, but I've never seen one."

"We've had a few at the ranch, but they've always been scared off. They don't want to fight humans. They want food." He brushed his hand along her hair. "The problem is you sat on the sand and lowered your head. They go for the head and neck. I panicked."

"No, you saved me."

He tucked his arm in hers. "Let's get to the car. I want to call the police and tell them what we saw, and then we need to talk."

Her legs still trembling, Alissa leaned on Ross as they made their way to her car. Ross stopped and made the call and then took time to call Fern. After he told her Alissa was fine, he handed Alissa the telephone to finish the details, but before she hung up, Ross took back the cell phone.

"We'll drop off her car, but we won't come in if that's okay. I want to take Alissa for a ride."

A ride? The reality of what had happened exploded in her senses. Alissa wanted to calm down. She wanted to go home and take a shower.

Ross clicked off and turned to her. "I hope it's okay. We need to talk now."

"Here on the beach?"

"No. Let's get out of here. This place is making me nervous. I don't know where that cat went, and I can't concentrate while I stand guard."

She nodded, realizing his suggestion made a lot of sense. "But I can't go anywhere fancy."

"Nothing fancy," he promised.

Ross started the car and made his way to Ocean View. Alissa parked her car then settled into his. She studied his profile, speculating on what could be so important. It probably had to do with the time he spent at his ranch or maybe another lecture about not walking alone on the beach.

Ross slipped his hand in hers, his expression uneasy. "I still can't believe what I saw. I'm glad you didn't see him and try to run. He would have been on you in a nanosecond."

"Don't say that. You're scaring me."

"Alissa. It's true. I watched the cat's tail twitch, and he crouched then inched forward toward you. I could have lost you, and I'm not willing to do that."

"Lost me?" She shook her head. "I can't believe I was so dumb, and you endangered your own life for me."

"For *us*. I couldn't bear the thought of anything happening to you." He drew her into his arms and rested his cheek against her hair. "It wasn't stupid. You didn't know a mountain lion had gotten so close to the city. It's always wise to go jogging with someone. Never alone."

"But I wanted to think. I needed time alone to make decisions." She felt his hand twitch in hers. "They were good thoughts, Ross."

"Good?"

She nodded. "I'm trusting in God's guidance, and I'm trying to make wise decisions."

"Tell me." His gaze searched hers for a moment before he straightened and shifted into reverse.

Alissa glanced away. "You first."

Ross released the brake and rolled to the end of the driveway. "Let's wait until we get there." He backed out onto Ocean View and shifted into drive.

Alissa didn't speak, confused as to where they were going and why.

Ross passed Forest Avenue, and when he reached Seventeenth Street, he drove into the parking lot and turned off the motor.

Her hands felt clammy. "This is Lovers' Point Park. Is this where you wanted to go?"

He nodded, slipped from the driver's seat, and came around to open her door. "I thought this was a good place to tell you what's been on my mind."

Lovers' Point. She felt swept away by his words. She'd spent a couple of hours thinking on the beach and had been struggling with her thoughts before that, but her talk today with Fern had made all the difference. As if the Lord had whispered in her ear, the answer came, as sweet as nectar to a monarch butterfly.

Ross wrapped his hand around hers and led her to a quiet place on the grass away from another couple a long distance away. He spread his jacket on the ground, and they sank onto it, close to each other's side.

Ross entwined his fingers through hers. "You want me to go first?"

Alissa nodded, almost afraid to hear what he had to say.

"I found a buyer for Prospero Vineyards."

Her head snapped toward him. "You what?"

"A neighboring vineyard has wanted my land for years. We've been in competition, but we've still remained business friends. He's offered me an overwhelming price."

Her pulse tripped through her veins. "What will you do?"

"I still own the avocado ranch, and that brings in a great income, too, Alissa."

"I hope you didn't do this because of me."

"You know I didn't. I did it for me, and for my fathers—both of them."

"Both of. . ." It took her a moment to understand. "You'll be blessed, Ross. It bothered you, and when we feel we're doing something not to the Lord's liking and stop it, then He will reward us."

He squeezed her hand. "God's tremendous gift of salvation is all the reward I need."

"What will you do now?" Her spirit sank, picturing his loss. "Move down to San Luis Obispo, I suppose."

He captured her gaze and grasped her other hand. "That depends on you, Alissa."

She let his words sink in.

"Say you're ready to give our relationship a chance."

"I do want to."

His excitement appeared to heighten. "I want to take you someplace tomorrow if you're willing. It's important you see this."

Alissa lifted his hand in hers and kissed his knuckles. "I've been doing a lot of thinking, Ross. When you left a few days ago, I had a horrible feeling of emptiness. I missed you, and I thought I'd pushed you away with my negative attitude. Your mom is always so upbeat, and she talks as if she thinks we're already a couple."

"She does."

His quick agreement made Alissa chuckle. "And I don't want to disappoint her."

The brightness in his eyes faded.

"Or disappoint myself," Alissa added, wanting him to know how she felt.

"You scared me for a minute. I don't want you basing any decision on what my mom wants."

Alissa slipped her hands from his and clasped his cheeks. "Do you really think I would?" She leaned forward and brushed her lips on his.

He looked surprised and drew her closer, lengthening the tender kiss.

"Fern thinks like your mom."

"Really?" His gaze drew her in, and a faint grin curved his lips. "Are you telling me you're willing to make this work?"

"I'm telling you. . .I am."

"Alissa." He opened his arms and drew her into them, kissing the top of her head, her forehead, and the tip of her nose. "I promise you we can make this work, because I know in my heart this is God's will. Everything has worked out too smoothly to be otherwise."

She smiled at him. "Do you want to know what I've been thinking?"

"Please."

"I thought about the butterflies and how God guides them, and I realize God will surely guide our steps, too. Another thought came to me after that. Fern loves the inn. She's willing to work longer hours and give me time away, and I've been thinking about that. Since she and I have talked, I see where I've gone wrong. I discouraged her in many ways. She continued to work at the inn because she needed the money, but what she really hoped was to be part of the business with me and help me make the inn a success."

Her heart skipped as she faced her admission. "Can you believe when I was thinking of what God wanted of me, I heard a verse from Ecclesiastes in my head, 'Better is the end of a thing than the beginning thereof: and the patient in spirit is better than the proud in spirit'? The beginning part of the verse was easy to understand, but when I thought about the last part—'the patient in spirit is better than the proud in spirit'—I blamed Fern for the pride, and it was me all along. I was prideful of the gifts God had given me rather than thankful for His blessings. I just ran along with my head in the clouds, doing everything and treating my sister like hired help—maybe worse, because she's my sister and I should have shown her love."

"But things are different now."

A weight flew from her shoulders. "I want Fern to manage the inn for me."

Ross's face brightened with a broad smile. "That's a great idea. Tremendous! You've been thinking all of this since I left?"

"Yes. Since you left. I didn't want to lose you, Ross, and I asked myself which was more important—the inn or you—and I decided."

He sat beside her, his face expectant, waiting for her to finish, and she couldn't wait to tell him.

"I want you with all my heart."

"Thank You, Lord," Ross said, looking at her with love in his eyes.

"But now I feel bad because I've put you under all this stress. You could have kept—"

"Alissa, without trying to, you motivated me to do something I should have done a long time ago. I love this area. It's far more beautiful than San Luis Obispo, and you'll still want to be part of the inn."

"I would still love to help out here. I love this place."

"I know. So believe me when I say God is in charge. What's happened is His will and not something we thought of by chance." He brushed his finger along her cheek. "Ask Fern if she can take over tomorrow just for the morning. We'll be back. I want to show you something."

"Can you give me a hint?"

"It'll be more fun if you wait."

She stuck her lip out in a playful pout, but her heart leaped with happiness.

❧

"Close your eyes." Ross hoped to distract Alissa before she looked at the view.

She frowned. "Why?"

"Because I asked you to." He put his arm around her shoulders. "It's a surprise."

"I hate surprises."

"You'll love this one."

She stared at him without blinking, and though Ross figured they would have a standoff, she finally closed her eyes.

"Now keep them closed." He moved the car forward into the circular driveway and parked. "Keep them closed."

"I heard you the first time," she said in a tone he recognized as irritation trying to sound lighthearted.

He walked around the car and opened the passenger door. "Step out, and I've got you."

She felt the door handle and slid from the car, grasping his arm.

"A few steps and you can open them."

Shifting her in front of him, his arms around her from behind, Ross told her to open her eyes. He felt her draw back when she saw the house. "What is this?"

"It could be my new house in Watsonville."

"Watsonville?" She spun around to face him. "Watsonville is less than thirty miles from Pacific Grove."

"That's right. Would you like to see inside?"

"I can't wait. Is the house inland, or can you see the ocean?"

"Come along, and you'll see." He took her hand and drew her up the short incline to the front of the house, its broad windows looking out over the landscape, the rolling hills and strawberry fields, some of which he would own soon.

"I love the big windows." She glanced over her shoulder to look at the view. "It's lovely, but it would be extraspecial if it had an ocean view."

Ross could see her disappointment so he didn't respond. He unlocked the door, and Alissa stepped inside.

"Ross, it's huge, and it's empty."

"But not for long if I buy it."

She hurried through the broad foyer into the living room with its elegant fireplace and built-in cabinets on each side of the mantel; then she made her way into the formal dining room and into the bright kitchen with golden-oak cabinets and counters. "It has a huge island. I love this. You could make wonderful meals here."

"I could?" She'd never tasted his mediocre cooking. "You mean Carmelita."

"Would she come with you?"

"I wouldn't move without her."

He took her hand and led her across the kitchen to the family room. "Now what do you say?" Seated on a hill, the landscape had its own small pond, and in the distance, the ocean spread out before them.

"Ross, this is unbelievable." She turned full circle. "I love all these windows where you can see the ocean, and this stone fireplace is out of this world."

"Carmelita has great quarters with a bedroom, sitting room, and bath beyond the kitchen. There's another suite where Mom can stay on the first floor, and upstairs are four bedrooms, each with a bath."

"What about an office for you?"

"There's a room that attaches to the garage with a door that goes out to a huge deck. Come and see."

She followed him, her mouth agape as she looked into every closet and opened every door. "I think it's a tremendous house. I really do."

"Could you live in a house like this, Alissa?"

She paused and turned to face him. "Who couldn't? It's wonderful with lots of room for guests."

He drew her closer, his arms around her waist, his heart in his throat. "And children. I think this house needs the patter of little feet."

"I have little feet." She lifted her foot and wiggled her tiny shoe.

"I'm serious."

Alissa gazed into his eyes, a look so sad it hurt him. "Isn't it too late for children?"

He nestled her closer. "Not if God's in charge. Forty-year-old women have children, and remember—a little one doesn't have to be my own flesh and blood to be my child. I'm leaving that decision to the Lord."

"Then I will, too," she said, a faint flush rising on her cheeks.

"Alissa, today is amazing. I love you with all my heart."

Her eyes searched his. "I love you, too, from the very bottom of my being. I never thought I'd say that, but it's so easy."

His chest tightened, longing to proclaim to the world that God had led him to this wonderful woman. "I've loved you forever."

"Forever?" A grin spread to her lips. "We've only known each other weeks."

"When God creates your soul mate, you've loved her forever. You only have to wait until He brings that special one into your life. It happened the day I met you."

He gazed at her sweet mouth, her lips waiting to be touched, and he lowered his mouth with a kiss he would remember always.

ૐ

Alissa spotted her sister with her handbag over her shoulder before she had a chance to talk with her alone.

"I think I'll get going," Fern said. "I checked a few things upstairs. The new cleaning girl is doing a good job, and I took care of a couple of reservation letters. They're ready for the mail in the morning."

"Fern, stay for dinner. When we were on our way home, Ross picked up some steaks to grill for us."

"Steaks? What's the occasion?"

Alissa glanced into the backyard through the kitchen window and saw Ross and Maggie deep in conversation. She assumed Ross was telling his mother their news; now she longed to shout it from the rooftop, but before she did that, she wanted to talk with Fern. "He's celebrating buying some new property and a few other changes in his life."

"Is that what he took you to see this morning? You were quiet about that, and I didn't want to ask."

"Yes. He's buying a strawberry farm in Watsonville."

"That's close to Pacific Grove." She stepped closer. "That's good news then."

"It is, and I hope this is some more good news." She closed the distance between Fern and herself then rested her hand on her sister's shoulder. "I want to ask you a favor."

Fern's face flickered with a question. "What kind of favor?"

"The kind I hope you'll accept. Let's sit for a minute." She patted a nearby kitchen chair and sank onto another one.

Fern rested her handbag on the table and sat, a frown growing on her face. "Is something wrong?"

"Everything is right, Fern. I've fallen in love with Ross, and I want to spend time with him. It's difficult to do that with all of the responsibilities here, so I wanted to ask you if you'd consider managing the inn. It would mean so much to me. You belong here as much as I do. It was our family home that bought this place, and I feel as if it's part yours anyway."

Fern's eyes had widened, but she hadn't uttered a sound.

"What do you say, Fern?"

"I'm speechless."

"I suppose you need time to think. That's arrogant of me to expect a decision so—"

"Alissa, stop."

Fern startled her, and she did just that. She pressed her lips together.

"I'm startled, but I'm thrilled—first because you've found the man of your dreams, and second because I would love to work here at the inn. Nothing would make me happier."

"Really?"

"Really."

Alissa rose and dashed to her sister's side, kissing her cheek.

Fern rose, and they embraced as the back door opened and Maggie came in using her cane. She looked rosy cheeked, and the grin on her face let Alissa know Ross had told her. Ross followed with the steaks on a platter. They both had surprised looks on their faces, from seeing Fern in her arms, Alissa guessed.

"I hope you're staying for dinner, Fern," he said, sweeping the platter beneath her nose. "You can't pass up a Cahill-grilled steak."

She chuckled. "If you insist. Anyway, how can I pass up the celebration?"

Ross did a double take from Alissa to Fern, and she knew he'd misunderstood.

Alissa chuckled. "I told Fern about your latest business deal."

"Ah," he said, looking pleased. "Are the salad and potatoes ready?"

Alissa nodded.

"Then let's gather around the table for a blessing."

They were seated and joined hands. When her fingers touched his, Alissa felt something fall into her palm, and her heart soared.

"Heavenly Father," Ross said, "we thank You for every blessing You shower on us, and we thank You for vacations that lead us on journeys we never expected. We ask You to bless this food and bless each of us here. And, Lord—" He paused a moment and released her hand.

Alissa understood. She opened her palm and gazed on the gorgeous glowing diamond set in gold filigree. She let out a gasp, and the two women looked up, their mouths dropping open; then they both smiled.

Before they looked at the ring, Ross continued. "Father,

we ask You to bless Alissa and me with Your grace and love. You've brought us together in an amazing way, and we thank You for the love we have for each other, for our families, and for You. We pray this in Jesus' name."

Amens rose heavenward as Fern and Maggie leaned closer to watch Ross slip the lovely gem on Alissa's finger.

Everyone talked at once as they admired the ring and asked question after question while the food got cold, but Alissa didn't care. All she could hear was Ross's voice earlier in the day saying, "I've loved you forever."

She would love him forever and to eternity.

epilogue

The Next May

Alissa couldn't believe how her life had changed since the evening a man and a woman arrived at Butterfly Trees Inn and she thought they were a May-December married couple. When she pictured the scene, she chuckled, now that she'd grown to love the man she'd assumed was Maggie's husband.

Maggie had become a second mother to Alissa, and though she wished her own mother could be with her for this special day, her joy couldn't be diminished. Today she would become Ross Cahill's wife. Two single people on separate journeys who met that amazing night as only the Lord could have planned.

Ross had jumped into the wedding plans like a colt in spring. They'd selected the Asilomar Conference Center. Alissa loved the fieldstone pillars and dark brown cedar-shake building, nestled amid the pines, with its sweeping porch and a view of the bay. It was not only a lovely setting, but also a reminder of the day she had faced the mountain lion and made the wisest decision of her life. Today she faced no lion. Instead she would face the man of her heart.

She and Ross had visited the facility to view the wedding chapel then selected the chapel hall for their dinner, and they even topped off their plans by choosing to honeymoon on the grounds in one of the center's lovely guest rooms, so close to home yet far away from their everyday lives. They could stroll the beach or walk the boardwalk across the sand dunes and watch the sunset on the bay, never alone anymore but always together as one.

Fern came through the kitchen doorway, wearing her blue dress, the color of a summer sky, and looking especially attractive with her new hairstyle. She'd changed since Alissa had given her more rein at the inn, preparing for her to take over. Fern had begun to care about herself, and it showed in her manner and in her appearance. Alissa praised God for opening her eyes and giving her another chance to make amends with her sister. Fern had moved into the inn the week before and taken over Alissa's quarters, while Alissa became a guest in her own house. She loved the new sense of freedom.

Though Alissa knew she could do the housework at the new home in Watsonville without Carmelita, she loved that Ross wanted her to have a housekeeper and wanted to give Carmelita a home. Alissa knew she could cook if she wanted and give Carmelita well-deserved time for herself. Having help in the huge house would allow Alissa free time to work at the inn for Fern, and it would give Alissa more time to be active in church and the community. It hadn't taken her long to realize, too, that being Ross's wife meant an active social life she would enjoy with him at her side.

Since Ross had moved to his new home, life had changed. They were only a short distance apart, and they'd begun to feel even more like partners as they planned their future. He'd asked her to select some new furniture for the house in Watsonville. Though she loved what he would bring from Paso Robles, she added a few pieces to make the place their own—including a gorgeous piece of artwork of the Pacific Grove beach, painted by a local artist. She would never be homesick looking at the lovely seascape with the waves dashing on the steadfast rocks.

Her life had been so much like those rocks. She'd stood firm in her faith, no matter how life's disappointments and troubles had dashed her hopes, and God had sent her a man with the same conviction.

"I can't believe this day is finally here, and I'm so happy for you," Fern said, standing back and shaking her head. "You look absolutely lovely in that dress."

"Thanks. It is beautiful," Alissa said, catching a glimpse in the mirror of the beaded bodice with the delicately draped neckline adorned with seed pearls. She smoothed the skirt of her gown, a swirl of beads along the sculptured skirt. A veil seemed unnecessary, and instead she'd selected a low crown of pearl and translucent beads, the same style that graced her dress. She gazed again at her magnificent diamond that glittered in the afternoon sun, shooting red and blue colors like fireworks. "I've wanted to show this gown to Ross so many times, but I stopped myself. He'll see it today, and that will make the wait worthwhile."

Fern drew closer and kissed her cheek. "The wait was worthwhile, wasn't it?"

Alissa knew the wait Fern alluded to. Waiting for marriage had allowed her to meet the man God had planned for her and one who was far more wonderful than she could have dreamed.

"It's time, I think. We'd better go," Fern said, beckoning her as she moved to the doorway.

Alissa made her way to the car and fell silent, overwhelmed by emotion, as they drove to the Asilomar center.

The scent of pines and warm grass greeted her as she stepped from Fern's car. They hurried inside past the large stone portals of the entrance, and she made her way to the area where she would wait to be called for the wedding.

Maggie had already arrived and stood inside, the small room beside the box with the florist logo. Alissa knew it held Fern's and her bouquets.

Maggie opened her arms, and Alissa hurried into her embrace, emotion heightening as the minutes ticked past.

"You look so beautiful," Maggie said, stepping to the table

and opening the florist box.

Alissa gazed at the woman she'd grown to love. "You look wonderful, too, and I'm thrilled to see you walking as you used to. I think of it every day. It's a miracle."

"I know," she said. "I was very blessed." She turned to Fern and lifted her bouquet from the box, a blend of white and pale rose-colored flowers tied with a sky blue ribbon. "Perfect. Look how it matches your dress."

Fern eyed the ribbon and her gown, agreeing the color seemed exact. She grasped the blossoms and lifted them to enjoy the scent.

"And now the bride," Maggie said, lifting a bouquet of white and pale pink lilies with tendrils of stephanotis trailing from a bed of greens. She handed the flowers to Alissa as a tap sounded on the door.

Fern opened it then closed the door again. "They're ready."

Alissa drew in a lengthy breath and followed Maggie and Fern from the room to the chapel hall where church friends, guests from San Luis Obispo, and even some from Paso Robles sat on white-draped chairs, waiting for the special moment.

Music from the Steinway grand piano across the room floated on the air, and Alissa watched as Maggie was assisted to the front and seated. Fern went first, looking lovely in blue, and Alissa lingered a moment, gazing at Ross, as rugged and handsome as any man could be with a heart that went on forever. When she took her first step, her gaze met Ross's, and his azure eyes drew her to him as if she were floating on a cloud.

Side by side, they listened to Pastor Tom's voice, praying for their life together, speaking the vows they repeated, and reminding them of the lifelong commitment they were making to the Lord and to each other. They exchanged rings, and Alissa waited for the glorious announcement that they were man and wife.

"Before we finalize these vows," the pastor began, "I ask you to follow the bride and groom outside where we will complete the ceremony."

Alissa's pulse skipped. *Outside?* She looked at Ross, confused and concerned, but he only grinned and took her arm. Her mind swirled with questions.

Ross took her arm and led her down the aisle between the rows of chairs, through the chapel hall, and out into the warm spring afternoon. A light breeze rustled the skirt of her gown, and the sunlight glinted from her diamond as she followed him onto the grass. Alissa gazed around the area for a surprise, but she found none. Nothing made sense.

Ross only smiled and patted the hand that was still clasped around his arm, and when the people gathered with them, Pastor Tom began again.

"In Genesis, we read how God created man and woman, saying man should not be alone. And in Noah's day, the Bible tells us Noah followed God's orders, gathering together pairs of all creatures that breathed to enter the ark. The Bible says, 'There went in two and two unto Noah into the ark, the male and the female, as God had commanded Noah.' Noah brought on board every kind of bird and everything with wings.

"Today we send Ross and Alissa onto their own ark on the sea of marriage, two becoming one where they will find shelter under God's wing."

Pastor Tom stepped back then motioned to a crate on the ground behind him that Alissa hadn't noticed. "Psalm 139 reminds us that God is always with us in every situation. 'If I take the wings of the morning, and dwell in the uttermost parts of the sea; even there shall thy hand lead me, and thy right hand shall hold me.'

"Today you will witness a special understanding of God's amazing promise to all of us, but especially as God shares this promise with Ross and Alissa. Standing here in Pacific Grove, we recall the monarch butterfly that travels miles and miles to reach safe ground for the winter, totally by God's design. We know as Christians we, too, must trust in God to reach the safe ground of our lives. Seeing the monarchs return brings us joy. With this release, you will witness the joy and unutterable emotion of the first moments in the new life of"—he spread out his arm toward Ross and Alissa—"Mr. and Mrs. Cahill."

A cheer rose as Ross drew Alissa into his arms, but instead of a kiss, he turned her toward Pastor Tom, who had knelt beside the box and lifted the lid.

Alissa let out a cry of joy as hundreds of butterflies—painted ladies, monarchs, and others—fluttered into the sky, their wings in colors of blue, teal, tawny browns, and orange. She watched their wings catch on the wind and lift high, just as her dreams and hopes had been caught on the wings of God's promises. Yet one lovely monarch fluttered near and rested on Alissa's bouquet. "Butterflies," she said with tears in her eyes. "Ross, look. God's sent us a special blessing."

Ross's gaze captured hers. "He has, Alissa. My wife. My love. My own lovely butterfly." His lips lowered to hers for a moment, a day, a lifetime that she would never forget.

While reading *Butterfly Trees*, you read about Alissa's cookies, including lemon bars, and Ross's special guacamole. I thought I would share Ross's recipe with you. If you'd like the lemon bar recipe, visit www.gailmartin.com, and you'll find it under the tab GAIL'S KITCHEN.

PRIZE-WINNING GUACAMOLE

Guacamole, which originated in Mexico, is a dip made from avocados. Make sure you check the ripeness of the avocados by pressing gently on the outside of the fruit, feeling for a little give. If the avocado gives too much, it is overripe.

Ingredients:
  2 ripe avocados
  ½ purple onion, minced (about ½ cup)
  1–2 serrano chilies, stemmed and seeded then minced
  2 tbsp cilantro leaves, finely chopped
  1 tbsp of fresh lime or lemon juice
  ½ tsp coarse salt
  dash of freshly grated black pepper
  ½ ripe tomato, seeded and pulp removed, chopped

Preparation: Cut the avocados in half. Remove seed and scoop fruit from the peel; place in a mixing bowl and use a fork to mash the avocado. Next add the chopped onion, chilies, cilantro, lime or lemon juice, salt, and pepper, and mash some more into a somewhat smooth paste. Keep the tomato separate until ready to serve. Cover with plastic wrap directly on the surface of the guacamole to prevent discoloration caused by the mixture being exposed to the air. Refrigerate until ready to serve. Just before serving, add the chopped tomato and mix.

Serve with tortilla chips. This serves 2–4 people.

A Letter To Our Readers

Dear Reader:

In order that we might better contribute to your reading enjoyment, we would appreciate your taking a few minutes to respond to the following questions. We welcome your comments and read each form and letter we receive. When completed, please return to the following:

Fiction Editor
Heartsong Presents
PO Box 719
Uhrichsville, Ohio 44683

1. Did you enjoy reading *Butterfly Trees* by Gail Gaymer Martin?
   ❏ Very much! I would like to see more books by this author!
   ❏ Moderately. I would have enjoyed it more if

   _____

   _____

   _____

2. Are you a member of **Heartsong Presents**? ❏ Yes ❏ No
   If no, where did you purchase this book? _____

   _____

3. How would you rate, on a scale from 1 (poor) to 5 (superior), the cover design? _____

4. On a scale from 1 (poor) to 10 (superior), please rate the following elements.

   _____ Heroine   _____ Plot
   _____ Hero   _____ Inspirational theme
   _____ Setting   _____ Secondary characters

5. These characters were special because? _____

_____

_____

6. How has this book inspired your life? _____

_____

_____

7. What settings would you like to see covered in future
   Heartsong Presents books? _____

_____

_____

8. What are some inspirational themes you would like to see
   treated in future books? _____

_____

_____

9. Would you be interested in reading other **Heartsong
   Presents** titles? ❏ Yes ❏ No

10. Please check your age range:
   ❏ Under 18   ❏ 18-24
   ❏ 25-34   ❏ 35-45
   ❏ 46-55   ❏ Over 55

Name _____

Occupation _____

Address _____

City, State, Zip _____

New Mexico
Weddings

3 stories in 1

Three grieving souls return home to Sweet Spring, New Mexico, and into the comfortable arms of family. Can the healing found in coming home help these searching souls to love again?

Contemporary, paperback, 352 pages, 5³⁄₁₆" x 8"

Heart♥ng

Any 12
**Heartsong
Presents** titles
for only
$27.00*

CONTEMPORARY ROMANCE IS CHEAPER BY THE DOZEN!

Buy any assortment of twelve
Heartsong Presents titles and
save 25% off the already
discounted price of $2.97 each!

*plus $3.00 shipping and handling per order
and sales tax where applicable.
If outside the U.S. please call
740-922-7280 for shipping charges.

HEARTSONG PRESENTS TITLES AVAILABLE NOW:

__HP541	*The Summer Girl,* A. Boeshaar		__HP614	*Forever in My Heart,* L. Ford
__HP545	*Love Is Patient,* C. M. Hake		__HP617	*Run Fast, My Love,* P. Griffin
__HP546	*Love Is Kind,* J. Livingston		__HP618	*One Last Christmas,* J. Livingston
__HP549	*Patchwork and Politics,* C. Lynxwiler		__HP621	*Forever Friends,* T. H. Murray
__HP550	*Woodhaven Acres,* B. Etchison		__HP622	*Time Will Tell,* L. Bliss
__HP553	*Bay Island,* B. Loughner		__HP625	*Love's Image,* D. Mayne
__HP554	*A Donut a Day,* G. Sattler		__HP626	*Down From the Cross,* J. Livingston
__HP557	*If You Please,* T. Davis		__HP629	*Look to the Heart,* T. Fowler
__HP558	*A Fairy Tale Romance,*		__HP630	*The Flat Marriage Fix,* K. Hayse
	M. Panagiotopoulos		__HP633	*Longing for Home,* C. Lynxwiler
__HP561	*Ton's Vow,* K. Cornelius		__HP634	*The Child Is Mine,* M. Colvin
__HP562	*Family Ties,* J. L. Barton		__HP637	*Mother's Day,* J. Livingston
__HP565	*An Unbreakable Hope,* K. Billerbeck		__HP638	*Real Treasure,* T. Davis
__HP566	*The Baby Quilt,* J. Livingston		__HP641	*The Pastor's Assignment,* K. O'Brien
__HP569	*Ageless Love,* L. Bliss		__HP642	*What's Cooking,* G. Sattler
__HP570	*Beguiling Masquerade,* C. G. Page		__HP645	*The Hunt for Home,* G. Aiken
__HP573	*In a Land Far Far Away,*		__HP649	*4th of July,* J. Livingston
	M. Panagiotopoulos		__HP650	*Romanian Rhapsody,* D. Franklin
__HP574	*Lambert's Pride,* L. A. Coleman and		__HP653	*Lakeside,* M. Davis
	R. Hauck		__HP654	*Alaska Summer,* M. H. Flinkman
__HP577	*Anita's Fortune,* K. Cornelius		__HP657	*Love Worth Finding,* C. M. Hake
__HP578	*The Birthday Wish,* J. Livingston		__HP658	*Love Worth Keeping,* J. Livingston
__HP581	*Love Online,* K. Billerbeck		__HP661	*Lambert's Code,* R. Hauck
__HP582	*The Long Ride Home,* A. Boeshaar		__HP665	*Bah Humbug, Mrs. Scrooge,*
__HP585	*Compassion's Charm,* D. Mills			J. Livingston
__HP586	*A Single Rose,* P. Griffin		__HP666	*Sweet Charity,* J. Thompson
__HP589	*Changing Seasons,* C. Reece and		__HP669	*The Island,* M. Davis
	J. Reece-Demarco		__HP670	*Miss Menace,* N. Lavo
__HP590	*Secret Admirer,* G. Sattler		__HP673	*Flash Flood,* D. Mills
__HP593	*Angel Incognito,* J. Thompson		__HP677	*Banking on Love,* J. Thompson
__HP594	*Out on a Limb,* G. Gaymer Martin		__HP678	*Lambert's Peace,* R. Hauck
__HP597	*Let My Heart Go,* B. Huston		__HP681	*The Wish,* L. Bliss
__HP598	*More Than Friends,* T. H. Murray		__HP682	*The Grand Hotel,* M. Davis
__HP601	*Timing is Everything,* T. V. Bateman		__HP685	*Thunder Bay,* B. Loughner
__HP602	*Dandelion Bride,* J. Livingston		__HP686	*Always a Bridesmaid,* A. Boeshaar
__HP605	*Picture Imperfect,* N. J. Farrier		__HP689	*Unforgettable,* J. L. Barton
__HP606	*Mary's Choice,* Kay Cornelius		__HP690	*Heritage,* M. Davis
__HP609	*Through the Fire,* C. Lynxwiler		__HP693	*Dear John,* K. V. Sawyer
__HP613	*Chorus of One,* J. Thompson		__HP694	*Riches of the Heart,* T. Davis

(If ordering from this page, please remember to include it with the order form.)

Presents

Great Inspirational Romance at a Great Price!

Heartsong Presents books are inspirational romances in contemporary and historical settings, designed to give you an enjoyable, spirit-lifting reading experience. You can choose wonderfully written titles from some of today's best authors like Wanda E. Brunstetter, Mary Connealy, Susan Page Davis, Cathy Marie Hake, Joyce Livingston, and many others.

When ordering quantities less than twelve, above titles are $2.97 each.
Not all titles may be available at time of order.

HEARTSONG
PRESENTS

If you love Christian romance…

$10.⁹⁹

You'll love Heartsong Presents' inspiring and faith-filled romances by today's very best Christian authors…Wanda E. Brunstetter, Mary Connealy, Susan Page Davis, Cathy Marie Hake, and Joyce Livingston, to mention a few!

When you join Heartsong Presents, you'll enjoy four brand-new, mass market, 176-page books—two contemporary and two historical—that will build you up in your faith when you discover God's role in every relationship you read about!

Mass Market 176 Pages

Imagine…four new romances every four weeks—with men and women like you who long to meet the one God has chosen as the love of their lives…all for the low price of $10.99 postpaid.

To join, simply visit www.heartsong presents.com or complete the coupon below and mail it to the address provided.

YES! Sign me up for Heartsong!